D1759712

burn the candle

ends.

finished!

60000 0001 66607

Published 2016
Copyright ©

Barry Buckingham has asserted his right under the Copyright, Designs and Patents Act 1988, to be identified as the author of this work.

This book is sold subject to the condition that it shall not, by way of trade or otherwise, be lent, re-sold, hired out or otherwise circulated without the publisher's prior consent in any form of binding or cover, other than that in which it is published and without a similar condition, including this condition, being imposed on the subsequent purchaser.

This is a work of **TOTAL FICTION**.

Names, characters, businesses, places, events and incidents are either the products of the author's imagination or used in a fictitious manner. Any resemblance to actual persons, living or dead, or actual events is purely coincidental.

Edited by OLBS (www.onlinebookservices.com)
Cover artwork created by Fayefayedesigns.

Other books by Barry Buckingham

Supernatural crime
The MW series
1 Manhattan Wolf
2 Solar Eclipse
3 Red Dawn

The Scalpturio series
1 The Beginning
2 The Pack

Military thrillers
The Hunt Trilogy
Scavenger Hunt
Man Hunt
Hunted

Adventure thrillers
Barracuda Jewel

2. Solar Eclipse

Chapter 1

The Bronx, New York.

Nate Williams was sitting in the back of one of his limousines with his son, Ross, excitedly chatting about the trip ahead, en route to La Guardia airport. The pilot for the family's, Bell 407, who'd been scheduled to fly them the short journey across the water, had rung in sick, so Nate and his son were taking the cross country route.

At the airport, their pilot was running through his pre-flight checks in the family's private Lear jet, ready to whisk them all off to Dallas for a Marvel convention. Ross' friends were already onboard, talking excitedly about the trip whilst they waited for him to arrive.

Ross loved all the superhero characters, Spider-Man being his favourite. As a birthday treat his parents had surprised him with tickets for himself and three of his friends to attend as VIP's for the weekend. The four of them had been talking about nothing else for months.

Driving the limo to the airport this morning, was Brad. He'd been working for Nate for twelve years and was counted as one of the family, Ross, even calling him Uncle Brad.

The normal route would have been to follow R87 and then across on R278, but this morning they'd been diverted because of road works and were now heading into the Bronx past the zoo.

"I'll take a short cut, Nate," Brad said, checking the in-car sat nav. "This traffic will take hours to clear."

Brad watched for a nod of approval from Nate in his rear view mirror and turned off the diversion route.

As they were heading around the back of the Bronx Zoo they came to a stop.

"Why have we stopped, Uncle Brad?"

Nate leant forward and looked out the front. "What's the problem?"

"There's a man laying down in the middle of the road. Shall I get out and see if he's okay?"

Nate glanced round at his son, who'd gone back to reading his Spider-Man comic, smiled and said, "Yes, Brad. Don't be too long though, we're due to take off in an hour."

Nate looked on as Brad went over to see if the man needed any help. He watched Brad kneel next to the man and then noticed someone run up behind him. Nate shouted a warning, but it was too late. The man hit Brad over the head. Nate went to get out to help, just as he spotted something being swung at his window. He jumped over his son to protect him as the glass exploded inwards, showering them both. Ross screamed as the two of them were pulled out and thrown to the floor, gagged and hooded. Nate had fought to get free but was coshed. Unconscious, he was thrown unceremoniously into the back of a waiting security van. Ross had struggled as well but was punched in the gut to shut him up, causing him to throw up in his hood before he was dumped on top of his father.

****

Brad groaned, then panicked. He tried to grab at the mask on his face but his hands were being held down by his side. He fought to get up, but his whole body had been restrained.

"Calm down, sir," a female voice said, gently, as a hand on his shoulder reassured him. "You're safe! You're in a rescue vehicle. Just breathe normally."

Brad tried to focus on the person talking, but the lights and sirens of the emergency vehicles that had responded filled the back of the ambulance, and his head. He breathed the oxygen in deeply, as his eyes began to focus. Then he was numbed by dread as the realisation of what had happened hit him.

Several days later, after no ransom had been paid, against the instructions of the FBI, two bodies were fished out of the Hudson. They were formally identified as Nate and Ross Williams. They were naked, and their throats had been slit.

After a short but swift investigation, Brad had been arrested. He was charged with being the mastermind behind the kidnapping. The pilot of the helicopter had been found dead in his bed, the gun that killed him being traced to Brad's father. And the roadworks that had diverted the limo had been bogus. To this day, Brad continues to protest his innocence.

Chapter 2

Several years later.

With the early morning sun breaking over the snow-capped mountains in the distance, Dave relaxed next to the pool and took another sip on his OJ. As he looked out at the picturesque view, he breathed in the heavy pine scent drifting off the nearby forest, the breeze that carried it across the plains had been warmed by the sun and was bone dry.

Dave loved coming back to the ranch, the clean air, no traffic, good friends, no work, but most of all... Linda! He smiled to himself when he heard her approaching from behind. Her musky odour, her gentle breathing and the beating of her heart filled his senses. He closed his eyes and listened to her footsteps.

Linda stroked her hand across Dave's shoulders and leant over him. "Good morning, handsome," she purred. She nuzzled the nape of his neck and sighed, "Do you have to go back today?"

"'Fraid so," he said, turning and kissing her. "The department won't run itself! Anyway, I'll be back in a few weeks."

"But I've hardly seen you on your own since you got here."

"Why not come back with me then? We could hang out, lunch, drink coffee, even visit some of your old stomping grounds, see how they've changed."

Linda looked at him for a moment and smiled. "Okay. I will!"

Dave watched as she walked, giving her bum a little wiggle, over to the edge of the pool and dipped her right foot in.

"The water's lovely," she purred. "Join me?" She reached back and unclipped her top, allowing it to fall to the ground. She stood, her eyes piercing Dave's. He swallowed hard and put his drink down, walked over to her and held her in his arms, her naked skin brushing up against his chest. Dave looked into her eyes, picked her up and stepped off the edge, plunging them both into the cool water. Linda squealed as they dropped off the edge, lifting her bottom to try and prolong the nip of the water on her skin.

When they surfaced, she grabbed his head and playfully pushed him down, Dave allowed his body to sink. Going limp, he slowly drifted up to the surface, floating on top, face down, like a rag doll. Linda nudged him, when he didn't respond she nudged him harder. She waited for a moment and when again Dave didn't respond she grabbed him and rolled him over.

"I knew you cared about me," he said, smiling. He squirted her with water from his mouth as she pushed him back under.

Later, the whole gang were standing around Dave's car to see them off.

Clayton said, jokingly, "Have a good time kids, stay away from the drunks and make sure you're in bed by nine o'clock!" Then he became serious, "Dave, Linda. Don't forget what's happening in the next few days. We haven't been around when it's occurred in the past so we don't know how it'll affect us! Okay?"

They both nodded. Linda blew them all a kiss as Dave drove off.

Chapter 3

Driving into New York, Linda sniffed the air. "Yep!" she announced, breathing in the car fumes and the odour of stale water mixed with sewage permeating up from the drains, "I haven't missed this place one little bit!"

Dave smiled, and stroked her leg, "Give it time. You've only been back ten minutes!"

Linda stared at the skyline and thought about the fabricated mixture of materials making up the skyscrapers as they got closer to the outskirts of Manhattan Island. Glass, concrete, wood, plastic, it was all there clogging up the view. She couldn't help thinking why she was heading back. She smiled as she looked at Dave, and thought, oh yeah!

The smog that shrouded the city on the calm summer days was all but gone as a gentle breeze brushed off the North Atlantic and up the Hudson River.

Heading over the bridge, Dave heard Linda sigh. He mused, this city slicker has gone feral!

As he drove over the bridge, looking down at the water, he suggested, "Tell you what, we'll get in, put on something more comfortable and go out to Grant's new place. We can stay the night if you want, go for a run along the dunes?"

"Let's not rush out there too quickly, I haven't had you on your own for a whole month!" she said, coyly.

Dave noticed how her eyes sparkled when she looked at him, he felt warm inside and fell in love with her all over again.

As they drove along Park Avenue, the traffic came to a halt. Dave hit his horn and cursed, making Linda laugh.

"Now this doesn't happen back home," she teased.

Crawling along, they passed some of the oldest family-owned money businesses in New York. The Spangler dynasty being up there with the oldest, now housed in one of the newer buildings. It stood a hundred floors high, the Spanglers occupying the top forty. Dave scanned the first twenty, admiring the mix of modern and gothic architecture, down to the sidewalk in front of the building. He noticed a group of men huddled together, by the underground carpark entrance, they seemed to be arguing about something, pushing a man in a suit. Dave thought about getting out but the traffic started moving quicker, so he had a last look, it'd all blown over, so he drove on.

As they approached the park, the traffic lightened and Dave had a reasonably clear run to his building.

Up in his apartment, Linda dropped her jacket on the couch and went over and helped Dave out of his. She took his hand, led him into the bedroom and pushed him down onto the bed.

Chapter 4

The day was still young, just after noon, so after a shower and a light snack, Dave and Linda set off for Grant's house down by the coast. His place was a little something he'd purchased after winning some money on the lottery, well that's what Grant was telling everyone anyway! He'd actually syphoned off one hundred and fifty $20k bundles from the drugs money case he'd helped Dave out with. Unknown to Dave, Grant had made three extra visits to the tunnel on the day they'd discovered the crates, filling a rucksack to the brim every time. He would have made four, but Dave finally noticed and started to get suspicious, so he quit while he was ahead.

As Dave turned off the main road onto Grant's drive, he felt his fangs start to extend. Linda looked at him and recognised the sign and turned her attention to the trees around the outside of Grant's property. Pulling up outside the house, they looked around as they got out and walked up to the front door.
"Can you feel that?" Dave asked.
Linda nodded, "Someone's watching," she said, as she scanned the tree line.
Waiting for the door to be answered, Linda held Dave's hand and smiled The warm air moving off the sea was covering them with the smells and sounds of the nearby coast.
A grin spread across Grant's face when he saw who was standing there. He came forward and hugged Dave, "Man, are you a sight for sore eyes! Come in, come in," he said, enthusiastically. As he closed the door, he scanned the trees, he could feel it as well. He turned and looked at Linda, and waited for Dave to introduce them. Linda could see Dave wasn't concentrating, so she held her hand out and performed

the honours. "Hi Grant, I'm Linda. Dave's told me so much about you."

"Pleased to meet you, Linda," he said, smiling. "Any friend of Dave's is a friend of mine." He turned and showed them through to the back.

As they stepped out onto the terrace, Dave spotted a young lady lying on a lounger near the steps at the far end of the pool where the sun was still fighting the shadows to stay in charge. She waved over to them and sat up as they went over to say hello.

"This is Max," Grant said, looking at Dave like the cat who got the cream. "She's been staying with me for a few days."

"Hi Max," Linda said, sitting down next to her. Linda smiled at Dave, and they sat down and started catching up on the last week.

Over a late lunch, just a light bite Grant cooked up on the BBQ, Dave asked Grant, "You stared out the door before closing it earlier. Everything okay?"

"I think there's someone watching me," he said, looking around at the trees. "I haven't managed to catch them yet, but I know they're there. That's one of the reasons I'm so glad to see you. Maybe you can help?"

"I got the same feeling as we drove up the drive. It also felt as if someone was watching when we walked into my apartment earlier. I'll have a look around later."

"Thanks, Dave. It'll put my mind at ease."

As Dave and Linda were driving off Grant's property, Linda asked, "Does he know about me?"

"I haven't told him, so unless he's guessed, then no. Do you want to come back later and go for a run?"

Linda smiled, "Oh yes!"

Chapter 5

Dave pulled up in an empty bay next to Grace's car, in the underground car park of his office block. When he got out, he smiled at the shiny red paintwork on her Mercedes. Dave had surprised Grace with the SUV after he'd come into "some money" when a drugs bust went pear-shaped a few months ago. He ran his hand down the side of the car, setting the alarm off. "Shit!" he cursed, as he flinched back.

"I hope you're not thinking of stealing that car, Agent?" Linda giggled, mockingly.

The alarm stopped shrilling about twenty seconds later, and the four-ways stopped flashing a few moments after that. Dave looked around the parking bays and then at Linda, "Shall we?" he grimaced, gesturing over to the lift.

As they ascended, Linda leant up against Dave and ran her hand over his chest. "If it wasn't for you, I would've never returned to the city," she sighed. Dave put his hands on her waist, leant in and kissed her tenderly. The bell sounded and brought them both back to reality. The doors slid open, and the late stayers coming back from their early dinners entered and took their places in front and around them, all heading back to their workstations for a few more hours. Dave and Linda had composed themselves and were standing next to each other, looking professional when the people entered. Dave returned the customary nods to his colleagues who made eye contact and stared at the ones who gave the questionable looks. Others glancing at Linda, smiling as if they knew her but couldn't place her.

As the lift worked its way up, Dave could smell the food and sweat odours carried on his colleagues' breath, hanging, trapped in the small compartment. Burritos, pizza, chilli, coffee, he gagged slightly and cursed to himself about his sensitive nose. One of the few downsides, he frowned. He glanced at

Linda and knew she was regretting it as well. Linda allowed her fingers to brush up against Dave's, causing him to flinch slightly from her touch. He responded secretly with his index finger, tracing it around her outstretched hand, up and down and in-between her fingers. She shivered as little shock waves cascaded up through her body.

As the other passengers disembarked at the different levels, Linda breathed in deeply, she couldn't wait to get out of the closed space, it was making her feel claustrophobic. The freedom of the forest and the open plains pulsed through her veins as she dreamed of being back in a few days. She hoped in the days to come she could convince her mate, Dave, to follow her for good.

"Hi!" Dave announced. Grace looked up at him and then at Linda, a smile broke across her face. "Linda. It's so good to see you. Are you coming back?" she asked, excitedly.

Linda shook her head, "No, I'm afraid not, Grace."

"Oh, what a shame! You'd be so good for this man," she said, smiling across at Dave.

"How are you and that catfish loving husband of yours?" Linda asked, affectionately.

"He's fine, still hasn't caught him yet. Probably never will!"

"I'll be in tomorrow, Grace," Dave said, "I've just come up to collect some things."

Grace nodded and smiled, then said, "Oh! The mayor wants to see you tomorrow at ten. And there's fresh coffee in the pot!"

"Thanks, Grace," Dave smiled. "I'll see you about lunchtime then."

"It's really nice to see you, Linda," Grace said, smiling as she watched them enter Dave's office.

Chapter 6

That evening, as Grant was sitting down with Max on the sofa, watching the highlights from the Masters at Augusta, he heard something out in the back garden. He sat up, dimmed the lights, peered out the window and watched as a shadow passed by the end of the pool.

"Are you okay?" Max asked.

"I am now!" he said, snuggling back into her. I am now.

What Grant hadn't seen was the second shadow follow on a few moments later, joining the first one up on the wall.

The two wolves glided around the end of the pool, the first one glancing at the person watching them from the window. With a single flinch, it leapt effortlessly and sat on top of the three-metre high perimeter wall. The smaller of the two followed a few moments later, ignoring the house, but stopping briefly to watch as the automatic pool cleaner drifted around on the bottom of the pool. It dipped and tasted the cool liquid, shaking its head at the chlorinated water before joining its mate.

Over five hundred pounds of pent up, controlled evil sat studying the trees. Their fur sucking in the darkness surrounding them, blending their huge hulks into the night.

With their eyes glowing red, green and blue from the ambient light cast by their celestial mistress high above, they scanned the blackness with pin-prick sharpness. Looking for movement, and testing the air with their snouts as they sat, invisible to all but themselves.

The normal noises from the wildlife subsided as soon as the two-night prowlers had materialised. Those outside their burrows, nests, dens, sets, or any place they called home scurried as quickly as they could to find safety.

The two wolves ignored the flurry of movement from below and in the trees and watched for the clumsy movement of their human prey.

The first wolf, the larger of the two, lifted its head and howled. The cry from its huge chest echoed, vibrating through the clear, warm night air.

Inside the beach house, Max jumped up and looked at the back windows, "What the hell was that?" she cried.

Grant calmly took her hand and guided her back onto the sofa. Max was shaking and staring at the window.

"It's probably just the local dogs. They've more than likely stumbled across an old carcase and are now digging in and feasting on it."

"That was no dog!" she mumbled, sitting as stiff as a board.

Grant stood, "Would you like me to go and check?"

She just looked at him, her eyes wide, "Are you crazy? That was obviously a wolf!"

"We don't have wolves around here!" he said, trying to sound blasé about it. Just then the two wolves howled together, this time making Grant jump. Makes sense, he thought.

Max jumped onto Grant and pushed him down to the sofa, she trembled as she buried her head in his shirt.

The two wolves moved swiftly and stealthily along the tracks between the trees that led down to the shoreline. Standing on the edge of the wood, they scanned the sandy beach. The big wolf looked at its partner and leapt forward, bounding towards the water. The other wolf waited a few moments, not sure, but then followed.

They ran along the shallows for a couple of kilometres, jumping rock pools and small inlets, rolling over each other in the water and on the sand. They passed a lone fisherman, quietly trotting past a few metres behind him, stopping to sniff at the bait he had in a bucket next to him. The fisherman shrugged deeper into his summer jacket, shivering for a reason he couldn't fathom. He looked around into the dark but the wolves were already gone.

Stopping at the base of a small cliff, they sniffed the air, not picking up any human scent, they morphed and stood, holding each other in the moonlight.

"I think I love you," Linda said.

Dave looked deep into her eyes and smiled, his fingers brushed the outline of her breasts, causing her to arch her back into him. Linda allowed his fingers to roam freely as they slowly sank down to the sand.

Chapter 7

The next morning, Dave stood outside the mayor's office. He took a deep breath, exploring the scent coming through the large wooden doors. Five. The mayor, a young lady - pregnant, and three men, one of them smelt the same as the young lady. Dave twisted his head slightly from left to right, pinpointing the position of each one of them.

He smiled, knocked and waited.

"Come in!"

Dave recognised the mayor's voice. When he entered, walking over to the mayor's desk, the mayor came round and held his hand out, Dave returned the gesture and shook it. "Good morning, Mr Mayor," he said, gripping the mayor's hand. It felt cool and firm. "A real leader," he thought. "Works out as well."

"Good to see you, Agent Phillips. Have a seat, please."

The mayor's PA was sat beside him. She was in her late twenties, slim and dark haired, no wedding ring, Dave noticed. He could feel the blood in her veins speed up as she scanned him, her breathing quickened to almost a pant. She blushed slightly as she caught his stare, immediately turning her head back down to her work. Dave smiled, inside he growled.

In the corner was a photographer, a young guy, who looked about the same age as the PA. "Same smell. Figures," Dave thought.

The young photographer looked at Dave and immediately looked at the PA and then back down at his camera.

The two other men took up positions about a metre behind Dave as he'd walked in, one of them closing the door. Dave flexed his shoulders at the threat but kept his wolf locked away. "Now wouldn't be a good time," he thought.

After their brief but positive meeting, Dave stood to leave, he shook hands with the mayor again, then turned to his PA and congratulated her.

She immediately looked at the photographer and coughed. "Excuse me?" she said, to Dave.

"The baby. Congratulations."

Her jaw dropped, she then shook her head, "I'm not pregnant!" she said, wincing at the photographer who was now staring at her.

Chapter 8

Just after lunch, Dave walked up to Grace and stood in front of her desk.

"Good afternoon, Dave," she beamed. "You look happy!"

"I've just been promoted," he smiled. "I'm now, the boss!"

Grace got up and hugged him, but looked a little sad, "Does this mean you'll be leaving us?"

"I thought you might've liked a pay rise yourself," he said, with a big grin.

Grace's face lit up, "Are we going up a floor?"

"Yep! But it's not official till tomorrow," tapping the side of his nose.

Linda walked out of her old office, just as Grace was putting Dave down. "What have I missed?"

"I'll be moving up a floor, and Grace is coming with me."

Linda hugged him, but inwardly it was the worst news she could have heard.

Dave went into his office and stood by his laptop. He took the top sheet off his notepad on the desk, scanned it quickly, crumpled it up and threw it at a small basketball hoop next to his aquarium. He watched as it hit the backboard and dropped through the hoop, cleanly landing in the trash can positioned underneath it. "Score," Dave mused.

Linda followed Dave into his office, turned and shut the door. Still facing it, she leant her forehead against the frame, "Does this mean you're not coming back to stay?" she asked, quietly.

He walked over to her and put his hands on her shoulders, gently turning her around. He looked into her eyes, "I'll be back once a month for a week or so. Now, though, with the promotion, I can come over in between as well."

She sighed, "I miss you, Dave."

He leant forward and kissed her, hugging her for a few moments.

"Coffee?" he asked.

She nodded, "Please!" Then without thinking, she switched on the lights and went and said 'Hi!' to the fish.

At her desk, Grace was on the phone to her husband, excitedly telling him the news. "Dave's been promoted, and he's asked me to go upstairs with him. We'll be able to get you that boat you've always wanted."

Moving closer to the watering hole was one of the things they talked about, going out on the boat and drifting lazily along, stopping and having picnics on the river bank. As they chatted excitedly about their future, a howl reverberated across the office floor. Holding the telephone to her ear, Grace flinched and slowly turned to look at Dave's office. She could see two huge shadows twisting grotesquely behind the blinds, she went to scream as the door splintered and the windows shattered.

Chapter 9

Grace's scream didn't even have a chance to leave her mouth as the first beast clamped its jaws around her face. Its razor-sharp claws flexed as they shredded her chest. Grace fought her attacker as it stood and lifted her out of her chair, feebly hitting the beast's flank with the phone.

Standing, its head scuffed the ceiling. It clamped down hard, shook once and tore the front of her head off. Grace's faceless body dropped back into her seat and sat quivering, her bottom jaw sagging. The top of her mouth, her nose and her eyes missing. Blood pooled around her chair as her life left her. The frenzied wolf bit into the flesh, shattering her skull, splitting it in two. It devoured one-half, discarding the rest before rampaging through the rest of the office.

Just behind, the larger wolf sprang at Grace's slumped body, its jaws open, its head huge and snarling with its fangs extending. It bit down on her right shoulder, picked her up and started slamming her down, tearing her to pieces and swallowing large chunks.

The handful of other agents who were back from lunch opened fire. Their screams muffling the sharp cracks from their weapons, their shouts echoing through the open-plan office as the two wolves rampaged. Snapping at the shooters, they gorged on whoever they could snatch, discarding limbs and organs in their wake.

The wolves headed down the stairwell, coming out in the underground car park. They howled as they smashed into cars and ripped lights from the ceiling. Smashing a door, they ran into a darkened room and went quiet.

Inside the blackened space, the wolves sniffed at the air, barging and snapping at each other. Suddenly the larger of the two stopped and fell to the ground, its body twisting and turning, shrinking as it morphed. The other one followed suit.

Chapter 10

Dave looked over at Linda and sat up, "Where are we?" he said, shivering, looking around, his eyes filled with confusion. He staggered out of the darkness, flinching away from the bright light.

Broken and dented cars were strewn all around, some of them turned on their side, fuel pooling around them, others with their alarms shrilling. Dave looked at the smashed ceiling lights and the trail of blood! "How? What?" he gasped.

Linda hobbled out, holding her side. Dave could see crimson coloured fluid oozing out between her fingers.

"What happened?" she gasped, looking at the wreckage.

Dave looked at her and watched as two small holes in her left shoulder closed up and disappeared. Linda followed his gaze and looked at her hands. She lifted them and screamed, as she stared at her intestines bulging out of her abdomen. As they watched, the wound rippled and pulled her organs back in, closing up as if it wasn't there.

Dave moved his hands up his torso and shuddered as his fingers went into his open ribcage, disappearing up to his knuckles. Linda cried as they watched the holes in his chest heal and the blood dry away. A few minutes later, Dave and Linda were both completely healed.

Dave looked at Linda and then down at himself. "Oh no!" he cried. He looked over at the gouges in the wall leading to the room they'd just come out of.

"That can't be all ours?" Linda said, looking in horror at the darkened red liquid running down the wall.

"We have to get out of here. We'll try to get back up to the office and act as if we were hiding," Dave said, looking around at the car park.

Walking along the backs of the cars, over to the lift, they were both mortified at the carnage. Linda started sobbing as she spotted what was left of an arm next to one of the overturned cars, "Those poor people upstairs!" Then she said, "Oh no, Grace!"

Dave went to open what was left of the door leading to the stairs but noticed their reflection in a car. It dawned on him that they were both naked.

As they stood looking at each other in the silence, they both flinched, Linda, screaming as metal started screeching and clunking. They jumped around and looked at the lift. The doors were shuddering closed. Dave went and held them, easily keeping the damaged doors open. Metal ground and groaned, creaking as it started travelling back up, jamming a metre from the top of the door opening.

"In here," Dave pointed. "The maintenance space under the lift has a hatch on one side. It leads to a tunnel heading towards the caretaker's workrooms."

"How did you know that?" Linda asked.

"Part of my anti-terrorist action plan, just in case the building was ever compromised." He jumped in, turned and helped Linda, then opened up the hatch door and crawled in.

"Only three other people know it's here: the boss and two maintenance men," he explained.

Dave could feel a draft blowing over him as he made his way towards a grill at the end, Linda followed close behind. He looked into the room below, shuffled round and kicked the grill out, listening as it clanged off the blue, painted concrete floor. They dropped into the room and sat on one of the benches.

"What the hell just happened?" Dave asked.

"I don't know," Linda said, trembling, her head in her hands.

The two of them sat looking around at the tool lockers and work benches with their vices bolted to the tops, lining the perimeter. A single large light hung above each work station. Brightly painted shadow boards covered the walls above each bench, each board holding a different array of tools than its neighbour. The room smelt of fuel oils and incense but was meticulously clean. On the wall, opposite to where they were sitting, Dave spotted a work rota.

With his enhanced sight, he could easily make out his office number with a note next to it: 'Broken extractor in washroom'. Under his name was also written: 'Check fish for food when Dave's away'.

Dave smiled at the last part and made a mental note to get the guys something special for Thanksgiving.

"We need to move quickly before we're missed," Dave explained.

They found some overalls in a locker and made their way back upstairs.

Chapter 11

Chaos reigned in the stairwell. There were people running up and down, weapons drawn, and others just staring at the marks on the walls. Dave looked in horror at the gouges running up over the ceiling. The walls were poured reinforced concrete, the scratch marks were big enough for him to put his fist into. Linda clung onto him, keeping close, avoiding eye contact with anyone.

When they got to Dave's office floor the two of them were prevented from entering by a guard. The guard spoke on his phone, looked at Dave and Linda and lifted his weapon. He indicated with a flick of his handgun to come in, ushering them over to Dave's office.

As they walked between the broken desks and dented and ripped filing cabinets, work colleagues were just standing, shocked. Some of them were in tears as they stood looking at the carnage. The open-plan office looked like an animal mortuary, waiting to be cleaned up at the end of a shift. The blood spattered around the room was still fresh, so there was no smell... yet!

Dave counted six bodies or parts of bodies, he couldn't tell. He dropped his gaze and shook his head as he walked towards his office door. They slowed as they drew level with Grace's desk but were prompted on with a slight shove from their guard.

As the two of them entered they both picked up on the scent of ammonia, it hung heavy in the air. Dave looked straight at where his aquarium used to sit, recognising the smell, now just a mess of dead fish and mottled plants. There was one piece of glass left hanging in the heavy duty frame. It had supported a small breeding box he'd installed a few weeks prior, to house the fish eggs he'd scooped out from the plants and rock crevices before the other fish feasted on them. All now gone.

As Dave scanned the wrecked room, he wasn't shocked at the level of damage, apart from his desk, which looked unscathed, everything had been smashed to pieces. The sofa had been ripped to shreds, his office plants were strewn across the floor, ceiling panels were missing and the walls had the same deep gouges in them. The part that had shocked them both was the damage to one of the floor to ceiling windows that overlooked the park, thirty floors up, now just a craze of broken glass held in its frame.

Their footsteps squelched in the sodden carpet as they stepped around the dead fish, some bitten in half, some shredded from the gills down.

Dave stopped and looked down at his oldest aquatic pet, a catfish named TC. Naming him after one of his favourite players, Tyson Chandler. Tyson had won the NBA defensive player of the year award in the two thousand and eleven season. Like Tyson, TC defended his little patch of rock furiously. Dave had attended every match that season, and after the last game was on a high, which, mixed with the four beers he'd had, found him walking into a pet shop and on impulse, buying the aquarium that sat proudly in his office...until today.

Dave bent down, stroked him and whispered, "Sorry TC."

"Sit!" Dave's boss ordered. "Agent," he said, to a man standing by the door. "Seal this room. Nobody in, nobody out. That includes you!"

Chapter 12

Dave and Linda squeezed together at one end of the sofa, next to where Dave's aquarium used to be. They sat fidgeting as their overalls soaked up the spilt water that had pooled in the indentations around the buttons in the leather covering.

His boss waited for the door to close and then held up their ripped clothes. He dropped them down in front of them and took his handgun out. The other agents already had Dave and Linda in their sights, their fingers flexing around the hand grips.

Both of them looked down at the torn, shredded rags at their feet.

As Dave looked up at his boss, Linda gasped, "Oh no, Dave!" as she stood and pointed out the window.

The agents in the room tensed as Linda stood. Some of the people killed in the office were good friends and they wanted to finish it, but they had their orders.

Dave followed her gaze and looked at the sun. "Oh God!" he gasped. "I'd forgotten about the eclipse."

His boss turned and looked at the moon slowly moving away from the sun. He put his weapon away and indicated to the others to do the same, but they didn't move. He looked at them and realised how close they were to firing, he decided not to push it and turned his attention to Dave and Linda.

There were five agents and Dave's boss in the room who'd just witnessed what had been seen outside the window.

Dave looked at his boss and dropped his head, "Where's Grace?" he asked, not really wanting the answer.

"She's dead! That mess outside your door is all that remains of her.

Linda slumped down and put her head in her hands and sobbed. Dave started to shake his head, his body started to tremble as a rage built up inside him. Looking at his boss, his eyes turned red as the wolf inside fought to get out. He screamed loud and long.

The five agents backed off slightly but kept them in their aim. Dave's boss, misguidedly, standing his ground.

Dave slumped down next to Linda, leaning back on the sofa with his hands pushed into his face. Dave's boss watched him for a second and started to relax, but once more he screamed out in rage and thumped his fists down on the leather. The five agents, and now his boss, stood line-a-breast, their weapons cocked and ready to fill Dave and Linda with every round they had.

When Dave had calmed down, his boss ordered, "Stand!"

Dave and Linda stood, both drooping their shoulders, totally spent.

"Get undressed."

"What?" Dave asked, thinking he'd heard wrong.

"Get undressed… Now!" training his handgun on Dave's head.

Dave looked at Linda and nodded. They both slipped out of their overalls and stood naked with their hands on their heads, as ordered.

"There isn't a single mark on you!" he gasped, as he walked around them slowly. "And I know you were each hit at least a dozen times, we counted them on the CCTV footage." He looked at the other agents, they were talking between themselves and staring at Dave and Linda. Dave's boss turned back to Dave, "Get dressed and sit down."

"What are you?" one of the other agents asked.

Dave looked at him and then at the others. He said slowly, "We're werewolves!"

This was followed by a slight murmur as the six men took the information in. Before they could say anything else, Dave followed up with, "What just happened, is something we have under control."

"That was under control?" his boss gasped.

"It's the first eclipse I've," he looked at Linda, "we've encountered. We didn't know this would happen."

"Why didn't you take precautions?" his boss asked.

"I forgot it was today!" Dave said, looking at him.

"We did! You have to believe us," Linda cried. "It totally went out of our heads."

"She was right!" Dave's boss mumbled.

"What? Who was right?" Dave said, looking at him probingly.

"She... Jasmin, was right," his boss said, staring at the two of them. "She was right about you. I just thought she was losing it and put it down to the stress of the job." He rubbed his face as if the problems of the world had been dropped in his lap. "So, how does it work... this... werewolf thing?" he said, articulating with his hands.

"A day before the full moon, we," Dave said, looking at Linda, "go into a secure area and morph. In the day we're normal, but at night we turn into the creatures you've just seen. We have no control over it once we change. Listen, boss, this can't get out. We'll have every nut in the country gunning for us. We have to keep it quiet."

Dave's boss looked at him, and then at his men, "Okay. This is now classified. It doesn't leave this room. We," he said, pointing to each one of his agents, "we're the privileged few. Understand?" He waited for each one of them to answer. "What now, Agent?" he asked Dave.

"It won't happen again until the full moon. Linda and I'll be at our secure hideout by then, locked away and safe from the outside world," Dave stopped and thought about what he'd just said and changed it to, "the outside world will be safe from us!"

The agents all stood staring at the two people on the sofa, each one of them not knowing what to do next.

Dave got up to walk towards the door and was immediately put in the sights of the six handguns that had slowly dropped as they had explained why. He stopped, and looked around at the men, "The moon's over, we'll not change now until the next full moon!"

"Sit down, Agent!" his boss ordered again.

Dave looked at him and shrugged, and joined Linda back on the sofa.

"Agent Lewis, clear the floor."

The agent nodded and walked out. The others left in the room could hear him ordering people out as they stood there looking at each other.

"Can I use the bathroom?" Linda asked.

One of the agents looked at her and smiled, "Sorry ma'am but you'll have to leave the door open!"

Linda nodded and thought, well they won't see anything they haven't already. "Thank you."

The agent clearing the floor opened the door and nodded. Dave's boss looked at Dave, "No surprises, Agent, otherwise, you'll have six times the amount of lead weighing you down!"

Dave winced. The look on the other agent's faces said it all, they were scared, and that made them trigger happy. "No surprises, sir."

The six agents watched the two of them walk across the room. Dave could feel their fear, he could smell the sweat pouring out of their skin, apprehension written across their faces.

When they opened the door, they went and stood next to Grace's table. A tear appeared on Linda's cheek. "Poor Grace. She wouldn't have stood a chance," she muttered.

Dave looked at the phone hanging down the side of Grace's chair, he could hear someone talking. He picked it up and listened. Grace's husband was on the other end, Dave could hear him asking if she was still there.

Dave's boss took the phone and explained there'd been an incident in the office and someone would be round to speak to him straight away. After hanging up, he turned to Dave, "My office, one hour, Agent," he said, quietly, looking around at the dead, dismembered bodies.

As Dave turned to leave, his boss said, "Agent. You're suspended until I've had time to think. When you get back we'll talk about how this is going to go down. Agent Maxwell and Agent Marks, here, will be accompanying you. If you decide to run they'll shoot you both, dead! Clear?"

Dave nodded and then looked at their chaperones'. He grimaced as he picked up the fear and hate permeating from their bodies. "We won't run, sir."

Across the park, a camera was clicking from the window of a hotel that faced the building Dave and Linda were standing in. The man taking the pictures was smiling. He said to himself quietly, "I've got you now, you devil freaks!"

Chapter 13

Dave's boss stared at the two of them as they walked back into his office. Dave and Linda were clean and dressed. Linda shuffled in her seat, wishing she'd never left the ranch.

"Okay, you two. What happens now?"

Dave glanced briefly at Linda and shrugged. "Your call, boss."

"Right, the way I see it, it can go one of two ways. We could throw you in prison, cut you into little pieces to find out what makes you tick."

Dave grimaced when he said this.

"Or we can work with it. Your choice." He stared at the two of them and waited for a reply.

"Before Jasmin was killed," Dave said, "we'd decided to work with it, and as she'd obviously told you, then let's carry on with that."

His boss looked at him and smiled. "Coffee?" he asked.

They both declined. Linda just wanted to leave and go back to the ranch. Dave just wanted it all to be over so he could get on. He looked at Linda and held her hand, he could see she was struggling.

"Agent."

Dave looked at his boss and waited.

"If you put a foot wrong you'll be shot on sight. You and Linda killed six good people today, so by rights, you should now be hanging from the rafters, but..." he looked at each of them, "you've been given a second chance. We need to find a way of using this..." his boss paused, "let's call it a talent. Until then, you'll tread very carefully. Understand?"

Dave nodded.

Linda was sent back to Dave's to rest, but Dave was ordered to go down to the thirteenth precinct to look into a money-laundering case that had been uncovered. The promotion he'd been given had been removed and he'd been placed directly under his boss, answerable to no one else.

Chapter 14

As **Dave entered** the thirteenth precinct, his eyes adjusted quickly to the reduced light. As he passed through the automatic doors he winced at the smell of rotting fish coming from across the entrance foyer. He looked over at a scruffy looking guy sat on a chair in the corner, reading a book. They'd placed him under a window and positioned a fan so it wafted the stench out. The guy caught Dave's eye and nodded, Dave returned the gesture and look away, hoping he didn't get up and come over.

The other people who were visiting the precinct were sat, leaving a space of about three chairs between them and the fish man, all complaining to the desk sergeant.

"Dave! How you doing buddy?" a familiar voice greeted him. "We don't normally see you down here."

"I'm good thanks, Lou. How's that wife of yours?"

Lou patted his midriff, "Still making the best doughnuts in Manhattan!"

Dave smiled at his larger than life friend.

"Hey, Dave," Lou said, taking him to one side. "Word has it a wild dog or something has just run riot through your building!"

"We had… a problem, but it's now contained," Dave said, patting his sidearm under his jacket.

This seemed to appease Lou. "Your case is in interview room four, third floor."

"Thanks, Lou." Dave looked over at the fish guy under the window.

"Comes in two or three times a week, you get used to the smell after a while," Lou said.

"Say 'hi' to Brenda for me. And take it easy with those doughnuts," he said, patting Lou on the shoulder as he turned to the stairs.

Dave mused at the speed of information sharing around the precincts, shame it's not that fast when we're after someone!

As he made his way over to the stairs, he was bumped by a man who was struggling with two officers. He'd broken free and ran straight into him. Dave turned and grabbed the man by the scruff of the neck, literally stopping him in his tracks. Using his strength, he held the man so the toes of his shoes were just rubbing the floor. He pulled him close to his face and growled.

"Watch it, arsehole!" the man shouted, shying back slightly as Dave's growl vibrated through his head.

Dave just smirked at him and apologised, "Sorry, sir, and have a crap day. Oh! You already are."

"Wise arse," came the reply.

Dave stood and watched, as the man was wrestled to the ground. He was then lifted, face down and placed in an empty cell to cool off. Dave returned the attempt by the man to intimidate him as he was taken away by giving him a friendly little wave as the door slammed closed on him.

Once the noise had died down, Dave climbed the stairs to the third floor.

Chapter 15

Later that evening, in a small bedsit overlooking Prospect Park, above a twenty-four seven convenience store, a young lady and her boyfriend sat around the kitchen table, staring at a small stick perched on top of a box.

The apartment was well furnished and warm. It had a well-stocked wine store, a full fridge, a state of the art entertainments system, and a selection of XXX dvds. The bedroom was bright and comfortable and decorated with a selection of classy erotic pictures. Around the bed, and attached to the ceiling, was an array of photographic gear, all remotely controlled.

The tension in the air could have been cut with a knife as the two of them watched a blue line appear.

As the young lady stared at the indicator window, she thought, "God! Let me be pregnant." She glanced at the young man and smiled.

He sat there thinking, "Please let it be negative. I'm too young for this shit!"

The two of them met at a nightclub three years ago. Their relationship started the same as any other young couple, texting, emails, letters and flowers turning up on their doorsteps, or at their place of work. They dined out together every night and spent much of their waking hours in each other's bed. She thought the relationship was going somewhere when he gave her a key to his apartment over dinner one night. She'd moved in, and was happy and settled. Then he'd started suggesting they experiment with their bedroom play, inviting strangers back with them after going out on drinking binges. She was reluctant at first but found she'd enjoyed some of it, and as she was in love with him she went along with it. And unknown to him, had come off the pill four months ago.

The blue line turned into a plus sign.

"I'm pregnant," she smiled.

"Fuck!" he thought. "How did he know?" the young man gasped. He got up and fetched a bottle of red wine, sat down and poured two glasses. "I thought you were taking precautions?"

"I am... I might have missed a few!" she said, looking down at the table. "What are you doing?"

"Having a drink!"

"I'd like an OJ, please."

The young man looked at her for a second and then smiled. When he sat down again, he said, "We're getting rid of it, aren't we?"

A tear welled up as she looked at him, not believing what he'd just said. "I thought this is what we wanted?"

Taking another mouthful of his drink and topping the glass up again, he mumbled, "It's what you wanted."

She looked at him, suddenly seeing him for what he was. She stood up, picked up his bottle of wine and poured it over him, and left.

Chapter 16

Later that night, as Dave laid back in his tub, savouring the hot water as it lapped over him, his eyes closed and his thoughts drifted away. Linda coughed. He cocked his head and looked at her standing in the doorway.

"I hope you haven't used all the hot water," she cooed. "Room for a little one?" she asked, dropping her towel.

"Always room for you, beautiful," he said, sitting up.

Linda leant back against his chest. Dave took a bottle of hot coconut oil from the shelf. She dropped her head forward and groaned as his powerful hands went to work on her neck, shoulders and arms. Working the oil into her skin, his hands drifted up and down her arms, around her slender neck and back across the line of her collarbone. She flexed her shoulders, encouraging him to go lower with his hands. He didn't disappoint her. His fingers brushed across the top of her breasts causing her to shudder gently. Her hands moved up and down his legs, squeezing his thighs. She rolled over and faced him, feeling his excitement as she kissed him slowly.

****

The next morning, Dave stood in the doorway of the bedroom and watched Linda as she slept. He admired her long legs, allowing his eyes to walk up her thighs, following the line from the wisp of pubic hair up to her navel. He stood mesmerised as her breasts rose and fell with every breath. He could feel her heart beating slowly as he watched.

He leant across the bed, kissing her on the forehead. Stirring slightly, she rolled over to her front but didn't wake. The sun's rays breaking through the mist that hung over Manhattan, flooded in through the window, bathing her naked body in warm sunlight.

"If she asks me now to go with her, she'd have me," he thought. He shook his head and left for work, leaving a little note stuck to the fridge door next to a picture of a rose.

Dave went via the diner, stopping for a coffee and a bagel. As he entered, Iris gave him a warm smile.

"No matter what sort of day she's having you can always count on Iris to smile," he smiled.

"Usual, lover boy?" Iris called, as he walked up to the counter. He nodded and put a twenty down. "Thanks, Iris. How's today going?"

"Good. I haven't been shouted at yet, and all the tips have been reasonable. Work?"

"Yep," he nodded. "I'll bring Linda round later."

She smiled, "It'll be good to see her, it's been a while."

"Thanks," he said, gesturing with his coffee as he turned and left.

Stepping out onto the sidewalk Dave got the feeling he was being watched. He looked around at people, making it obvious but couldn't detect anything, he did make out the agents following him though.

The man's camera clicked away, taking five photos in close succession as he smiled about taking him down.

Chapter 17

As Linda was clearing Dave's clothes off the floor, she put them up to her face and breathed in his scent, then tossing them in the laundry basket, she went off to meet him for lunch.

Once they'd eaten, they set off to meet with Grace's husband. Dave sent the two agents a text, detailing where they were going. He asked for some distance and said he'd be back in two hours.

Dave hailed a cab. Opening the door, "Madam," he smiled, bowing slightly as he let Linda in first.

"Gracious, sir," she replied, allowing her hand to brush his as she got in. She shuffled over to the other side and leant against him as he joined her.

"North Riverdale, Douglas Avenue, please," Dave told the driver.

As the cab pulled away from the kerb, Linda's skin tingled as she picked up a scent inside the vehicle but couldn't place it. She looked at the driver in the mirror, but couldn't place him either. Shaking her head, she pushed it out of her mind.

Dave noticed the agents as the cab pulled away, they nodded and pointed at their watches, then drove off in the opposite direction.

Grace had lived just outside Manhattan, across the river on the west edge. Dave had been over a few times for dinner, so when the cab made a turn he didn't recognise he got his phone out and checked on the traffic news. Not wanting to barge in on the driver if there were any traffic problems reported. Seeing it was clear, he leant forward and asked why the change in direction. When the cab driver ignored him, Dave tapped on the safety screen to get his attention. When this didn't work, he growled and punched the security screen, pushing it out of its housing onto the driver. Linda jumped at the unexpected show of force. The driver screamed and brought the car to a halt. He turned to confront Dave but jerked back. Dave felt his fangs retract as he took his badge out and pushed it in the driver's face. The driver made a break for it, running down the road, leaving his cab running in the middle of the street. Linda went to get out, but the door was pushed closed, knocking her back onto Dave. A man, wearing a black balaclava, slammed a hammer into the window, shattering it over the two occupants. He pushed a sawn-off shotgun through, up against Linda's chest.

Linda froze, the muzzle of the weapon digging into her ribs. She could see the man's finger twitching on the trigger. "From this range, it would literally cut me in half," she thought.

"Give me your money. Now!" the voice rasped, loudly.

Dave thought about going for his handgun, but looked at the end of the barrel and instead took his wallet out... real slow! As he handed it over, he let out a low growl. He could feel the fur coming through the skin on his back. He looked at the man's eyes, he was young and scared. The man looked at Dave, blinked, and snatched the wallet from his hand, he then turned and ran.

Linda breathed out, and they both got out of the cab shaking themselves down. They looked at each other and then up and down the deserted side street.

Dave motioned for them to walk back the way they'd come. He said, "I'd love to see his face when he finds my badge in there."

Getting another cab was easy, the lunch rush had finished and the cabs they were hailing were heading back into the centre of Manhattan.

Al, Graces' widower welcomed them in, asking them to sit, and offering drinks. Linda teared up as she thought about how kind he was being in the wake of what had just happened.

"How did she die, Dave?" he asked, staring straight into his eyes.

Dave looked at him and then at Linda. "There was an incident in the office. Grace got caught up in the crossfire. I'm sorry, Al. We tried to save her."

He nodded, and then asked, "Did she die in pain?"

"No. It was quick and painless," Dave explained. "She wouldn't have known anything about it." He wanted the ground to open up and swallow him whole, he was lying and hated himself for it.

Linda fought to hold back her tears, her heart was heavy at the loss of their good friend.

They stayed for an hour talking about, Grace, and the plans the two of them had, and about moving closer to their kids when she retired in a few years.

The journey back to the office was done in silence, with Linda weeping silently onto Dave's shoulder.

Chapter 18

The office floor was back to normal, all the blood had been cleaned up, but there was the smell of fresh bleach everywhere. New tables and partition walls were in place or being installed. One of the five nodded and tapped his sidearm as Dave entered, Dave grimaced at the thought of what might happen if the agents thought they were becoming a threat to them.

As Dave entered his office the phone rang, it was his boss informing him his wallet had been handed in at a police station over on the Bronx. "It's clean of any prints so you can go and collect it whenever you want. And your badge has gone."

"Thanks, boss."

Linda stood near the window, looking down at the trees in the park, "I can't wait to get back to the ranch. I think I'll go tomorrow!"

Dave nodded.

"Will you get another fish tank?" she asked, turning and walking over to the new sofa.

"No. I'll stick a plant there, less looking after."

Linda clicked her fingers and sat up, "I know where I've smelt that before. On your clothes!"

Dave looked at her quizzically, "Smelt what?"

"When I picked your clothes up this morning, I detected a scent I knew wasn't you, I dismissed it straight away, but then I smelt it again in the taxi."

"Loads of people wear the same cologne!"

"This was body odour, sweat. The taxi driver had it on him."

Dave thought about where he might have picked it up. The man at the police station. "I bumped into someone at the station who'd been arrested," Dave said, as he picked up the phone, "I'll ring them now and see if they're still holding him."

A few moments later, and it was confirmed he was still being held. The two of them set off for the thirteenth precinct.

Chapter 19

Grant was out next to the pool, a bit later than normal due to Max keeping him up most of the night.

As he lay there, his attention was caught by a flash of light reflecting from a tree at the back of the garden. Sitting up, he stared at a small box in one of the trees. Without taking his eyes off it, he walked over to the part of the wall that was under the tree. As he looked up, it stood out like a sore thumb. "Why the hell didn't I see that before?" he thought. "Max," he called. "Can you bring me the ladder from the garage?"

She stuck her head around the side of the doorframe, "What was that?"

"The ladder. In the garage. Can you bring it over, please, darling?"

Max smiled and pecked him on the cheek as she held the base of the ladder.

"What was that for?" he asked, with a smile. "Not that I'm complaining!"

"Just for being you," she said, staring at him. She watched his bum as he wobbled his way to the top, wolf-whistling as he took the steps slowly. Once he was at the height of the box, he worked his way through the branches to the trunk. Climbing the tree was harder than he'd bargained for, plus it was oozing sap, he was covered in the sticky fluid. Once he was within grabbing distance, he took hold of the camera and ripped it away from the branch, tucked it into his pocket and climbed down, brushing up alongside Max as he stepped off.

"Grant!" she moaned.

"It'll wash off, darling."

He smiled, as she whipped off her bikini top, went over and dived into the pool.

****

As Dave and Linda were leaving, the phone rang.

"Dave, it's Grant. I've found a camera in one of the trees!"

"Shit! Where is it now?"

"In my hand. What do you want me to do with it?"

"Can you bring it over to the office?"

Grant looked around at Max, as she pulled herself out of the pool and towelled herself down. "I'll be there as soon as I've finished up here," he smiled.

Dave put the phone down and looked at Linda, they then went up to see his boss.

In the boss's office.

"Okay. You need to find this person or persons, and bring them in. If you're right about what the camera might have on it then we don't want that recording ending up in the hands of the press. If it does shows you…. doing your stuff," he gestured with his hands, "then we'll have a real problem."

"The camera will be here shortly," Dave nodded. "I'll see if the boys in the lab can get a trace from it."

His boss buzzed through to his secretary and told her to expect Grant then looked at Dave, "Okay. Any news on the money laundering?"

"It's small time. A couple of grand at the most. It's just been blown out of proportion by the Chinese whispers."

His boss nodded.

Dave added, "But I think I may have stumbled across the taxi robberies that have been eluding us for the last few months, and I think the gang leader is in custody down at the thirteenth precinct."

"How'd you come across that?" his boss asked, sitting back.

"It was Linda. She picked up on a scent in the taxi earlier, it matched the scent on my clothes she'd put in the washer this morning. When I went over where I'd been to have any contact with anyone, I narrowed it down to the thirteenth precinct yesterday."

His boss looked at him and gestured for him to sit down and Dave filled him in on what he had.

"It's all yours, Agent. Let's see what this... gift of yours can produce." He turned to, Linda, "Linda, or can I call you, Agent?"

"I'm afraid not. I gave this all up when this happened to me... us. I'm leaving, and I won't be coming back." She looked at Dave when she said this, sadness on her face. "I'm sorry, Dave. I can't do this anymore. The call of the wild is too strong. Will you come back with me?"

He shook his head, and held her hand, "Sorry, darling, I belong here. But I'll be back every month."

"That's a shame, Linda," Dave's boss said. "Having two of you on the force would wipe out the crooks in no time! You take care, okay." He got up and offered his hand, "Goodbye."

As Linda got to the door, Dave's boss said, "Linda."

She turned and looked at him.

"Don't leave the country, alright?"

She recoiled slightly at this.

The two of them left the building and headed back to his apartment, this time there were no agents in tow. Linda packed her bag, and Dave took her to the airport. Once her flight had taken off, he turned and headed for the Thirteenth Precinct.

Chapter 20

On one side of the table, in the middle of the room, sat Dave and Lou. On the other side, sat the man he was going to question, and his lawyer.

"Ready?" Dave smiled.

The lawyer looked at his client and nodded. Dave turned the recording machine on and went through the usual routine of introductions before they started the interview.

"Okay, Mr...," Dave looked at the brief sheet in front of him, "Remoras. How many taxis have you robbed?"

"Don't answer that." The lawyer looked at Dave and frowned.

"Okay. Where do you operate from, you and the rest of your gang?"

"Officer. My client's here because of an alleged burglary. You can't ask him any questions about any taxi robberies."

Dave smiled at Remoras and sat forward, ignoring the lawyer, "Does he wipe your arse as well?"

Remoras jumped at Dave, and swung a long sweeping arm towards him, hitting the lawyer instead, knocking him forward and banging his head on the table.

Dave, quick as a flash, pushed Remoras' head down next to his brief's and whispered into his ear, "Now we have that on video... Remoras," as he cuffed him.

Remoras' lawyer got up and rubbed his forehead. He looked at his client and walked out, leaving him face-down on the table, spitting curses across the surface.

Dave sat for a few moments looking at Remoras, then said, "You scratch my back and I'll scratch yours."

Remoras looked at him, and then at the sergeant.

"I'll spell it out for you, shall I? Help me and I'll get the judge to shorten your sentence."

"Screw you!" he spat.

"Okay," Dave said, calmly. "Have a nice time in jail!" He got as far as opening the door.

"Okay. Okay."

"Good." Dave sat down and explained really slowly what he wanted him to do. When he walked out, he stopped at the door and turned back to Remoras. "If you double-cross me," he stopped and looked at the other officer, "Is that tape off?" he asked.

The sergeant nodded.

"If you double-cross me, I'll rip your throat out!"

Remoras was about to tell him where to get off when he noticed his eyes change colour. Remoras made the sign of the cross and nodded.

Chapter 21

The two wolves sat looking out across the calm North Atlantic Ocean, the only movement was the shallow rise and fall of the late summer swells drifting in from the open sea. The moon, halfway through its cycle, was shining brightly behind them, casting their shadows far out across the open water.

They breathed in the salty air, as one of the wolves morphed and Dave laid back on the warm sand. His heels just within reach of the swell drifting up the beach. His hand stroking the other wolf's fur.

The other wolf laid down and placed its head on Dave's chest and morphed. Hugging him, Linda asked, "Why don't you want to come back, Dave?"

He looked up at the stars, "I love the forest, and being with you, but I need more. I need the city!"

Linda turned her head and looked at his throat, watching as his Adam's apple rose and fell as he swallowed. She sighed, "I miss you."

Dave stroked her head and sat up. "I'll race you to the lighthouse."

Linda rolled off him and morphed, bounding along the water's edge towards their goal, Dave hot on her tail, letting her lead. As he ran along behind her, he thought he heard something growl above him. When he glanced up, a dark cloud, darker than the darkest night, had formed above them. Red flashes briefly illuminated the sky as the thunder rolled from it. Dave felt a sense of foreboding flood through his heart. Fear pulsing through his veins as he dropped his head and whimpered. He hadn't felt like this since being bitten.

Dave sat up quickly, he was sweating, his sheets drenched. He looked around his room, the low glow of the nightlight bathing the room in a calming blue sheen. He thought of Linda.

Slumping back onto his pillow he looked at the clock on his bedside table.

"Two am. I wonder if Grant's awake."

****

As Dave strolled up to Grant's house, the security lights came on, a moment later Grant stood at the door with a shotgun.

"Whoa there Grant, FBI!" Dave called.

Grant dropped his firearm and hurried him over.

"What's the panic?" Dave asked.

"There was someone creeping around here earlier, taking pictures of the house. They came up the drive but left as I came out the door."

"Did you recognise them?"

"No, but it freaked Max out. She's talking about leaving."

"Where's she now?"

"She's upstairs taking a bath."

"Okay. Show me where you saw this guy."

The moon was casting its night light, sending long eerie shadows through the copse that surrounded Grant's property, its tendrils fingering every nook as it hunted the ground. The sunset chorus had long quietened as the night was taken over by the night critters, chirping and buzzing, but they had now gone quiet, sensing the wolf.

They stood by the gate, leading up to Grant's house, chatting about the camera.

"Nothing found yet," Dave said, "but the lab has got a few more tests to do. We should know by tomorrow morning."

Grant nodded and looked up at the moon. Dave smiled as he watched the uncertainty spread across Grant's face.

"Two weeks to go, Grant."

Grant looked at him and smiled nervously.

Dave stood and breathed in, long and deep, tasting the air, it reminded him of the woods back at the ranch. The fauna and flora scattered among the trees, mixed in with the woodland critters, were all giving off their own musky odour. Dave thought it was weird, as he should be able to at least pick up on the cologne the person was wearing. "Are you sure they came this way?"

Grant nodded and picked up a few flowers to take back to Max.

"I'll stay for a few minutes and look around. If that's okay with you?"

Grant looked at him, and nodded, as Dave started to undress. "Oh! I'll see you inside," he said, turning and scuttling hurriedly back up the drive.

Dave smiled and slipped his pants off.

"Dave!" Grant said, turning back to him.

"Yes!"

"Is Linda... you know," he shivered, and looked around cagily, "... a werewolf?"

"Yes. A very beautiful werewolf."

Grant smiled and hurried back indoors.

As the wolf glided stealthily through the trees it caught a slight scent, near the back of the house where the camera was found. Ammonia, nitrocellulose, wood smoke. It was right on the edge of its ability to pick it up. "No wonder I couldn't smell it earlier," Dave thought, having morphed to pick up a fragment of clothing.

The Wolf dropped down flat, Shit! It worked its way back to where Dave had left his clothes, morphed and dressed. Dave ran up to the house. Inside, he told Grant to close all the curtains. "I found a scent. At first, I didn't realise where it came from, then it hit me. The woods around the ranch. The person who set the camera knows about me... us!"

"Knows about you? What's wrong with you?" Max asked, stepping back towards the wall.

Grant and Dave stopped and looked at her, Grant spoke first.

"We were involved in something the government did, it was closed down because of the controversy around it. But there are a few people who still won't let it go."

Dave looked at Grant and smiled.

"Oh," Max said. "Is it dangerous?"

"No," Grant smiled, as he went over and held her hand. "It was just risky for the people who were involved." She seemed to relax as Grant led her over to the sofa.

Dave got his phone out and spoke with his boss.

Chapter 22

The next morning, Dave walked through the doors of the thirteenth precinct and straight into a barrage of photographers taking his picture, and reporters shoving microphones in his face. He stood back, shielding his eyes from the close proximity flashes popping, and looked over at the desk sergeant.

"What's going on?" he shouted across the room, as he pushed a camera back at a young man who'd caught his cheek in the shuffle.

"Hey, man!" the cameraman squealed.

Dave looked at him, and calmly said, "How about I arrest you on a felony charge?"

"I'm just doing my job, man."

"So am I."

The desk sergeant shouted back, "Some loony has reported seeing a werewolf, and says it was you!"

Dave laughed, and pushed his way through the crowd of cameras and recording devices over to the desk.

"I need to see Remoras."

"He's been released."

"Why?" Dave scowled.

"Technicality. Something to do with you making a false arrest and bruising his face in the interview room. His brief is backing him up on it."

"Shit!" Dave cursed, under his breath. "Do you know where he's gone?"

"Really, Dave! You're asking me a question like that."

"Take a wild guess!"

The desk sergeant looked at him and said sarcastically, "His mother's!"

Dave emerged from the back of the building and hailed a cab. He climbed in, "Bronx Zoo."

As the cab pulled out from the side street bordering the precinct, he glanced towards the entrance to the station, and for some reason looked up at the building opposite. A flash caught his eye as he scanned the windows. When he looked harder, he could see the long lens of a camera moving in and out as it focussed on his cab. "Stop!" Dave shouted, to the driver. He threw him forty dollars and jumped out. He looked up at the window, the lens was gone. Dave ran over and entered the lobby, straight over to the stairwell.

As Dave made his way up the stairs, towards the fifteenth floor where he'd seen the camera, the hairs on the back of his neck started to quiver. He picked up his pace and took the steps four at a time, bounding effortlessly up the flights. He stopped at the eighth floor and listened, he'd heard a door above him open. He waited for the person to come down, thinking it was the most likely route out for the cameraman to leave, then the door slammed shut. He caught a scent on the air, Wood smoke. My apartment! "It's him," he growled.

He raced on, almost leaping whole flights in one go, his claws extending and digging into the walls to help pull him forward quicker. He burst through the stairwell door and looked up and down the hall. The well-lit corridor was clean and clear, then he heard the bell ring on the elevator and saw the arrow above the doors signalling down. Dave headed back down the stairs, briefly glancing along the hall at the lift on each floor.

When he emerged on the ground floor, he walked calmly over to the lift and waited.

He took a deep breath, but couldn't pick up on anything except... lavender!

As the bell sounded the lift's arrival, Dave stood in front of the opening. He shook his head as an old lady pushed past him, leaving the compartment empty. Lavender, he thought, as his eyes smarted at the strength of the odour. He stuck his head in and checked all the walls. "Damn!" he snarled. He turned and ran back up the stairs.

When he got to the fifteenth level he went along each one of the doors taking deep breaths until he found the one he wanted.

Standing to the side, he moved his hand over to the handle, twisting it slowly. He took a deep breath and allowed the door to pop open an inch on its seal.

The scent he'd picked up earlier, and at his apartment, wafted out through the door. He waited for a second and then pushed the door fully open with his foot.

The single room was lit only by the sunlight coming through the open window at the far end. Dave listened, nothing! He holstered his weapon and walked in.

Looking around, Dave spotted mud under the window where the person holding the camera had been standing. He went over and crouched beside it. Taking an evidence bag out of his pocket, he scooped a few pieces up, held the bag up to the light and stared closely at the colour. "That's ranch soil," he said to himself. He peered out the window down at the entrance to the police building, then at the window opposite to the one he was standing behind. He could see straight into the canteen. That's exactly where I was sitting when I was speaking to Doug earlier, he thought.

He scoured the rest of the room and came to the conclusion it had been used just for the photos.

Chapter 23

Down in the foyer, Dave tapped the plunger twice on the bicycle bell sitting on the counter top, the bell boy looked up at him and smiled. "Yes, sir?"

"Room one-four-four. Have you got a name for the person who used it today?"

"Probably!" the bellboy smirked.

Dave looked at him and pulled his badge out, "Do I need to ask you again?"

The bellboy frowned and tapped a few keys on the laptop in front of him. Dave smiled as he walked out of the hotel, but had it wiped off by a camera flash less than two metres from his face.

The young man, Dave had spoken to earlier stood smiling at him. Dave recognised him from the mayor's office. He sighed as he hailed a cab. Jumping in, he instructed the driver to take him to the Bronx Zoo, the long way round.

"What do you mean, the long way?" the cab driver asked, turning to face him.

"Go around the park."

The driver looked at him and said, "That'll be a hundred!"

Dave gave him the money and sat back. He glanced around a couple of times but couldn't pick up on a tail. As the cab approached W97th Street, he asked him to stop. He got out and walked into the park towards the tennis centre.

Dave sat down, looked around at the trees and thought about the ranch. A few moments later the young reporter came around the corner of the tennis pavilion and stopped in his tracks, Dave sat there watching him.

He beckoned him over. "I've got you a Coke."

"Erm, Thanks!"

"Okay, what do we have here? A reporter following an FBI agent." He left it there and waited for a response.

"I'm not following you, I'm having a walk in the park."

Dave cocked his eyebrow and stared at him.

The young lad didn't know where to look. "Am I under arrest?" he asked, timidly.

Dave played on the immaturity of his prey, "Not yet, but if you keep following me you will be."

The reporter picked up his drink and took a long swig, he then asked, "Can I go?"

"Will I see you again?"

"No, sir."

"Then you can go." He watched him finish his Coke and get up. "How's that young lady of yours? The PA from the mayor's office."

"We broke up."

"Didn't want the responsibility, eh?"

The young man sat down again and look at Dave. "So, how did you know Carrie was pregnant?"

"Intuition," Dave said.

The young man nodded and stared at Dave. "Are you a werewolf?"

Dave choked on his drink, "A what?" he gasped.

"A werewolf. Are you?"

"Do you work for a serious paper?"

"Freelance."

"Well you're going to be freelance for a long time if you keep thinking like that," Dave smiled.

The young man recoiled slightly at the thought and then thanked Dave for the drink and left. Dave watched him go. If he's thinking like that then so are others, he frowned.

Dave looked around at the park and over at the area where his friend had been shot. He lifted his glass.

****

"Where's Agent Roberts?" the voice boomed through the intercom.

"Nobody's seen him since this morning, sir."

"Find him, quick!"

"Yes, sir." Dave's boss's secretary picked up her phone.

"Yes, Lynn?" Dave answered.

"He's looking for you, and he sounds cross."

"He's probably just found my resignation letter."

When Dave said this, Lynn went quiet. "Are you leaving us, Dave?"

"Yep. I'm getting out while I can."

There was a pause, and then, "Can we meet?"

"Meet?" Dave said, a bit taken back by the request.

"I know what you are," she whispered.

Chapter 24

Dave opened the door of the diner and was greeted by the smell of ham and eggs and coffee. He went over to his usual chair, smiling at Iris. Her eyes sparkled as she returned the gesture, Dave was her favourite customer.

Dave had been a regular at the diner for the last ten years, stopping daily for his morning coffee and twice a week eating in the evening on the way home. He sat at his usual table over by the front, he liked to see what was happening outside. He ran his hand along the glossy orange seat, part of the interior of the old carriage, and edged over to the window. The old owner, Jack, use to tell him the seat was lucky. How he was sat on it when the Knicks won the NBA championships back in seventy and seventy-three, and how the money he won from the bet had paid his mortgage off.

The old carriage had been painted in the colours of the team, in celebration of their win. It had been removed back in the late nineties, to make way for the tower block, which now loomed above him. Pictures of the train the carriage belonged to hung above the counter, bordered by three Knicks shirts, framed and proudly signed by the winning team. Other pictures dictating the iconic era of growth and prosperity in New York filled the rest of the walls in the small café.

Dave looked at a picture of the Twin Towers opposite him, underneath was an inscription:

Not forgotten, forever in our hearts.

A poignant reminder of the dreadful day when so many good people lost their lives to a terrorist attack on the buildings. Now though, the diner was in the middle of a thriving money area of Manhattan, a stone's throw away from Central Park.

"Coffee, please," he mouthed.

Iris smiled and ran her fingers through her hair. She hoped one day he'd ask her out, but knew deep down she was thirty years too late.

"How are you today, Dave?" she let her fingers brush his hand as she placed his coffee down.

"I'm good. Are you still holding the nightshift up?" He noticed she looked tired and her hair was fading back to grey where she hadn't treated it.

"Yep. Burt still hasn't found anyone willing to work for the money he's offering, can't blame them though. I'd be out of here in the blink of an eye if I had enough to buy a small place down on the coast." She looked at him, "I don't suppose you've got a spare hundred thousand you could give me?"

Dave smiled and shook his head and watched as she turned away to serve a couple of customers at the counter.

Dave rang Grant. "Grant, meet me down on the docks. Where Jasmin's body was fished out under the jetty."

"Okay. When?"

"ASAP. I think I've found our photographer."

"Wow! That was quick. Who is it?"

"You'll see when you get there. Stay out of sight but somewhere you can hear. Bring along your iPad and record what's said, okay?"

****

Grant left his house, unknown to him under the scrutiny of a clicking camera. He felt the hairs on his arms stand. He scanned the buildings and trees as he drove out of his neighbourhood.

The cameraman was sitting on the hood of his car, up on a ridge approximately eight hundred metres away. He'd got the last of the pictures they needed and was now busy uploading them to their cloud account. These are going to make us a fortune, he smiled as he dialled a number on his phone.

When the person answered all he said was, "I've got them all."

"Good," came the response.

The call had been short, and straight to the point. The cameraman packed up his equipment and drove off.

****

Dave arrived at the Hudson about twenty minutes later, he hung around until he sensed Grant was near, he then worked his way to the meeting point. He deliberately made some noise as he approached.

Lynn heard him. "It's lovely, isn't it?" she said.

Dave stood beside her and looked over at the area where the aircraft came down a few years back, still amazed it didn't break up and kill everyone on board. He breathed in the salty, muddy odour breezing in off the water, he also picked up on the wood smoke coming from Lynn. He thought about the forest. Pine beats mud any day of the week.

"That was a hell of a landing!" he said.

"My brother was on the aircraft, said he'd never fly again, and to this day he hasn't. Drives everywhere now. Takes him bloody hours to get anywhere... idiot!"

Dave looked at Lynn. She was still an attractive woman, late forties. Married, no kids. She kept herself fit working out daily in the company's gym.

"Cut to the chase, Lynn," he grunted. "I didn't come down here to talk about your brother's psychological problems. What do you want?"

Grant had positioned himself below the level Dave was on, between the uprights. He was tucked into a service platform just above the waterline, holding his iPad above his head to catch what was said.

Dave could hear Grant breathing and smiled, but just hoped he had it turned on.

"We both know what you are," she said.

"What?" he asked.

She looked at him and backed up. "You're a werewolf," slowly retrieving her sidearm from her purse.

He looked at her for a second and then burst out laughing, "You're crazy. I'm out of here."

He turned to go, but she said, "We have pictures and video of you... changing."

He stopped and let out a heavy sigh. Turning slowly, he said, "What do you want, Lynn?"

"I want all the money you took from the drugs bust."

"No!"

"If you don't give me the money we'll upload the picture to YouTube."

Inside Lynn was a mess, she was trying not to show any fear but after what happened in the offices she knew he could rip her to pieces in the blink of an eye.

"We?" Dave said, taking a step towards her. He could feel and hear her heart thumping against her chest.

"If I don't ring in twenty minutes, he'll upload the pictures."

Grant heard Dave growl, he shrank into his jacket and closed his eyes. Although Grant had seen Dave change a few times he still thought it was the work of the devil, and it scared the shit out of him.

"They'll all think you're crazy and say you've just Photoshopped them."

"Are you willing to take the chance, Agent? There'll always be someone out there who'll believe them, and it only takes one to start the stone rolling downhill."

He looked at her. He could smell the sweat pouring out of her skin, her muscles trembling. The wolf inside him was fighting to tear her throat out.

"You'll be hunted down like the freak you are. They won't stop until they have you." She hadn't realised that he was slowly moving towards her, she staggered back, coming up against one of the posts as Dave stepped in close to her. Holding her breath she tensed, her back pressed against the upright, her handgun pushed into his gut. She wanted to scream and run, but her feet felt heavy and her legs were weakening more by the second. Her vision started to tunnel as the blood drained out of her head, but then Dave stepped back. He looked down at her weapon and smiled. He lifted his hand and stroked her cheek, she flinched at his touch, it was icy cold. She looked at his fingers, her eyes bulged as her deepest fears fought to get her mouth to open and let them out. She stared, standing rigid, as she watched a claw extend from his index finger, straining to turn her face away as he placed it on her cheek.

Dave drew it slowly down and around her throat. He smiled as the skin opened slightly, blood dripping onto her blouse. He sucked in the metallic odour from the red liquid as it oozed out of the wound. He wanted to rip her throat out and let her juices fill his mouth, he wanted to feast on her!

Lynn found her breath and screamed. She punched him away, dropping her weapon. "Don't touch me, you freak!" She looked down as her handgun slipped through the timbers in the deck and disappeared into the murky water below.

Feeling a warm, wet sensation on her cheek, she put her hand up to guard her face, expecting to have to hold the wound together. Wiping her cheek roughly she looked at her hand but was shocked that it was clean. She wiped again with the same result.

Dave smiled as he watched the wound close up and heal. "Welcome, Lynn."

"What have you done?" she stuttered.

"Now they'll hunt you down as well, so I suggest you tell me where the pictures are, or we'll both be in big trouble."

Lynn stopped and looked down at the floor, she took a long deep breath. "Who's that?"

"That's Grant. He's my friend."

Lynn looked up, tears flowing down her face. "Why?"

"I was protecting us."

"Us? There are more of you?"

"A few, and now you as well."

Lynn felt grief building up inside, then an anger forcing its way out. She leapt at Dave, but he was ready. He sprang forward and grabbed her in mid-flight and slammed her down on the beams. His wolf was superior in every way. The whole structure shook as the two of them grappled with each other. Grant whimpered as he shrank deeper into his hidey-hole.

Dave turned her over and place three sets of handcuffs on her wrists, he then took out a length of wire and bound her feet, tying them off on the cuffs. Lynn was spitting curses at him and pulling at the bindings, blood running from cuts opening and closing on her wrists and ankles.

"I've got her, boss. Bring the boat around." Dave looked down, "Grant, go home. Call Linda and Let her know what's happened. I'll be at my apartment later." He heard Grant scuttle away.

As the police launch drew up alongside the jetty, Lynn had half changed but gone no further. Her back end was a wolf.

"Are you okay, Lynn?" Dave asked, concerned.

She looked at him and bared her fangs, her eyes deep black in colour piercing his soul.

"There's something wrong," Dave said, to his boss who was now kneeling next to her.

His boss looked up at the five heavily-suited agents, "Get her in the box."

"Don't let her scratch you or bite you," Dave warned, as he took a hood out of his pocket and covered her head.
"Otherwise you'll be right next to her in the same box."

As the launch pulled away from the jetty, Lynn was howling. Dave looked at the box and tried to work out what was happening.

As they made their way up the river to the coast guards' building, Lynn went quiet. He looked at his boss and went forward to open the observation hatch in the top.

"Is this normal, Agent?"

"No, boss. I don't know what she's doing." Dave slid back the cover and recoiled at the sight. Lynn had disembowelled herself and was chewing on her paw, shredding it like tissue paper. "Shit!"

His boss leant over and had a look, he flinched back, turned and vomited over the side. Dave took his weapon out and opened the door to the box. He was going to fire but she'd stopped moving. He reached in and felt for a pulse, nothing. The stench coming from inside had one of the other agents joining their boss as Dave locked the box back up and sat down.

Chapter 25

"**S**hit, her phone!" Dave said, standing up. His boss looked at him, "What?"

"She had to ring her partner within twenty minutes or he'd put the film on YouTube." Dave opened the box as the others trained their weapons on what was inside it.

"Lynn!" Dave called cautiously. He felt for a pulse again, nothing! He rummaged through her clothes. "Found it." He went through the contacts looking for anything that jumped out at him. What stopped him was a single word, 'wolf!'

"Did you get the money?" the voice rasped.

Dave paused. He looked up at his boss who was talking on his phone.

"Did you get the money?" the voice repeated.

"Got him," his boss mouthed. "The SWAT team will be on him in eight minutes."

Dave waited for the man to ask again.

"God damn it, Lynn. Did you get the money?'

"No she didn't," Dave answered.

This time the man paused. Dave took the receiver away from his ear to check if he was still connected.

"Who is this?" the man eventually asked.

Dave said two words, "The Wolf."

Again silence. Then, "Shit! Where's, Lynn?"

"She's dead! Who's this?"

"You freaking freak!" the voice burst down the phone. "Where's my wife? You freaking son of a bitch!"

"She's on a boat with us. Where are the pictures?"

There was another pause, and then it was too late for Lynn's husband. Dave heard a window smash and the sound of a stun grenade exploding. Fractions of a second later, he heard the

SWAT team stamping through the building. He heard a muffled order shouted. "Put the gun down!"

Lynn's husband moaned, and Dave heard a single shot.

A few moments later, a voice on the phone said, "Agent Harris?"

"Yes," Dave answered, knowing what the officer was going to say.

"He's dead, sir."

"Thank you. Secure the building, we'll be over in thirty minutes."

Chapter 26

As Dave and his boss, closely followed by the other five agents, walked up to the house, Dave stopped. "This is the smell I picked up the other night at Grant's house, the ammonia and the smell of the woods around the ranch," he said, breathing in deeply.

"Let's hope we can put this to bed. We need to keep this contained," his boss said.

"Where's Lynn's body going?" Dave asked.

"To the morgue and then it's going to be incinerated."

Dave nodded, and then looked at the other five agents. "You guys okay?"

They just stood staring at him.

Inside the house, the man in charge of the SWAT team was stood on guard outside the door down to the cellar.

"Hi, John," Dave's boss greeted him.

John nodded, "Harry."

John looked confused and worried. "What's going on, Harry?"

"Who else has seen what's down here?" Harry asked.

"Just the two officers who cleared the room. They think it's some school prank. They're over there," he said, pointing.

Dave's boss waved them over and told them to follow them down.

Dave's boss looked at one of his agents. "Put someone on this door. Tell them not to let anyone in, not even the president!"

In the cellar, Dave's boss turned to John and the two officers. This is spiralling out of control, he worried. "This is now classified," he said, looking at the three newcomers.

The three SWAT officers looked at each other and nodded.

Dave's boss nodded at Dave.

Turning the monitor on, Dave stood back and joined the semi-circle of men now intently watching the screen come to life. The pictures that followed showed Dave at the ranch and his flat, changing and hunting. It also showed Clayton and the others doing the same at the ranch.

When the film had played through, the three SWAT officers looked at Dave and backed off. One of them mouthed something to himself and put his hand on his sidearm.

Dave saw him react and put his hands up in front of him, "Guys, you have nothing to fear." He went and sat down at the monitor and went online. "Anyone know much about YouTube?" he asked the room.

One of the agents came up and started searching, adding special codes into the search engine they use to track items. "They're not on there yet, Dave." When he realised he'd called him by his first name he sat motionless for a moment expecting a reprimand.

"Thanks, Mark," Dave said, patting him on the shoulder.

His Boss told John to clear the room, "Bag everything and get it up to my office."

John looked at his two officers, "Looks like we're cleaning up, guys."

Chapter 27

Later that night, Dave, Grant and Max were sat talking.

"I need a drink," Grant announced. He went over to his bar in the corner and sorted their orders.

"Smoothie for Dave, beer for Max and a small Bourbon for yours truly," he said, placing them down. He went and stood next to the fireplace, raised his glass and slung the shot back. He grimaced as the hard liquor hit the back of his throat, burning slightly. "That's better," he sighed. He went and poured himself another.

"Busy day, darling?" Max asked.

"You don't want to know," he shuddered.

Grant looked at Dave and waited for him to say something.

"We found the person responsible for the camera in the trees. She's now dead, and so is her husband," Dave explained.

"That's terrible. Who was it?" Max asked.

"Lynn. My boss's PA."

"Who's your boss?" Max looked shocked when he explained. "FBI!" she gasped. She looked at Grant, "He's FBI?"

"Yep," Grant nodded.

"We're not all dark horses going around in buff coloured raincoats and black trilby's," Dave joked.

Max stared at him for a second, inwardly thinking to herself whether she'd paid her last three parking tickets. A little light flashed in her head and she turned to, Grant. "Are you…?" she probed.

Grant shook his head, "No. I'm just helping a friend."

Later, as Dave was leaving, Grant asked, "Do you want to join us for dinner tomorrow night? My treat."

"Thanks, Grant," Dave nodded "See you about seven?"

Grant nodded and watched as Dave got in his car before closing the door.

Chapter 28

With the moon high in the clear night sky, the two wolves ran along the sandy beach, jumping dunes and rocks, darting in and out of the shallow surf with the sea breeze stroking their fur as they headed towards the lighthouse.

The young photographer Dave had spoken to walked around Dave's car, taking photos of their clothes on the back seat.

The young man was neither warm nor cold and didn't feel the cool sea breeze. His feet were bare, the sand pushing up between his toes. Nervously, he looked around at the trees, scanning for the two dog-like creatures he'd watched run off. Turning to leave, he froze, rooted to the spot as the two dogs howled. Their long, drawn-out screams echoing along the dark beach, causing him to retreat into himself.

Breaking into a run, the young photographer struggled against the pull of the sand, it clung to his feet, holding him back as he frantically made his way along the edge of the wood, back to the main road where his scooter was parked. Inside he was screaming, he kept looking around, thinking at any moment he'd be brought down and ripped apart by the two monsters.

Starting his scooter, he jumped on and raced off up the road, ignoring his helmet as it bounced off along the blacktop behind him. With the wind lifting the sand, he rode along the coast road unaffected by the coarseness biting into his face. He screamed into the city, back to the safety of the street lamps.

With the sound of the wolves echoing in his head, his body trembling and his mouth dry, he mounted the kerb outside his building. He dumped his scooter in the bushes and ran, tripping and rolling across the freshly turned soil in his attempt to get inside. Bursting through the main doors, clattering them off the walls, he ran to the elevator. He repeatedly pressed the call button, whilst eyeballing the main doors. His ears alert to the silence of the corridor. His heart hammering away in his chest as he waited for the doors to explode open and the deep darkness following him to breathe on his neck before it tore him to shreds.

****

Stuart woke, shivering in a cold sweat. He turned the bedside lamp on and rubbed his face. Looking around his bedroom, he frowned, bloody nightmare! This wolf story's getting to me. He looked at the empty space in the bed his girlfriend once used until she went and got herself pregnant.

He got up and poured himself a coffee and sat watching Sky News in the kitchen. The flash line across the bottom of the screen made him sit up.

'Are there wolves in New York?'

Stuart looked around the kitchen and listened to the rain on his window. Shaking, he went back to bed.

Chapter 29

The next morning, as Dave was blending his morning smoothie before his run, his phone rang.
"Agent Phillips?"
  "Yes, boss."
  "Meet me in my office in one hour."
  "Yes, boss." Dave hung up, picked his drink up and contemplated the day ahead. The run will have to wait, he thought, as he headed for the shower. When he'd finished he rang Linda.

****

"Morning handsome," Iris welcomed Dave. She smiled and stroked her hair flat as he sat down. "What can I get you?"
  "Morning, Iris. I'll have a coffee and some ham and eggs, please," he smiled.
  Iris turned and shouted his order through and then sat down.
  "Dave," she said, looking at him. "These reports coming through on the news channels of a wolf loose in Manhattan. Should I be worried?"
  "No," he smiled. He put his hand on hers, and said, "You're safe, Iris."
  She sat for a few moments, feeling the warmth through his touch and thought about what life could have been like, but the spell was broken by someone coughing at the till waiting to be served.
  "Thank you, Dave."

  As Dave tucked into his breakfast, he thought about the implications of people being scared, and the threat of every bounty hunter on the island out with their hunting rifles, all gunning for a shot at the wolf. I need to be alert. He sprinkled a little more salt and finished his breakfast.

****

"Have you seen what's on the news, Agent?" Dave's boss grimaced.

Dave nodded, "I had Iris down at the diner asking me if she'll be okay to walk home at night. What's the mayor saying about it?"

"He's putting a statement out at noon. He didn't want to, said he'd be playing into the hysteria of people's minds just talking about it. He's right though, it doesn't matter how much you say it's all been fabricated by the press, somebody out there is going to believe them." His boss looked at Dave across his desk for a moment and then asked, "Is it true, do I need to be worried... about you and your little gang, Agent?"

"No, sir. What you saw happen with the eclipse only happens with the full moon.... normally!"

Dave's boss nodded and sat back. "Okay."

"I think everybody must be talking about the bear that escaped from the zoo."

His boss looked at him questionably. "Bear!"

"The one we shot last night. I can get a picture off the internet."

"Good thinking. I'll let the mayor know."

As Dave left the boss's office, he picked up on a scent in the hall that he recognised. When he got to his office door, his new secretary informed him he had a visitor.

Dave opened the door and looked at Stuart sitting down at the window, admiring the view. When Stuart heard the door open, he jumped up and turned and stared at Dave.

"Good morning, Stuart."

Stuart nodded and watched as Dave went and sat down. Dave could feel the young photographer's heart thumping, his breathing was deep and his eyes were wide as he came and sat down opposite Dave at his desk.

"How can I help you this morning?" Dave asked.

"I have some pictures of the Wolf."

Dave sat up and fidget slightly, "Pictures, of a wolf?" he said guardedly.

"No, not a wolf. The Wolf!"

"So why are you here talking to me. Surely your boss would pay you a lot to have them in his paper?"

"I had a dream last night."

When Stuart started with this opening line, Dave sat back and thought, "Why do I get all the nutcases?"

"I dreamt you were the Wolf!"

Dave let out a chuckle. "Okay. Let's say for a moment I'm the Wolf, which I'm not," he said, leaning forward. "Why are you here?" He could sense the apprehension in Stuart's movements as he put a folder on the desk in front of him.

Stuart twisted his head slightly and then fanned his jacket, indicating it had suddenly gotten very hot. Dave picked up on this and smiled, "I'm sorry I can't open a window, we're on the thirtieth floor."

Stuart looked over at the floor to ceiling windows involuntarily and swallowed hard.

"It's okay," Dave said. "We don't throw people out the window for coming to us with crazy ideas," he let what he'd said hang in the air for a few moments and then finished with, "Anymore!"

Stuart frowned and opened the folder in front of him, "This is you," he said, sheepishly handing him a photo. "And this is the Wolf."

Dave sighed and sat back. He smiled as he looked at the quality. "What's this supposed to prove? That you're good with

Photoshop!" as he slid them back down onto the desk and looked at him.

"I'll take them to the press with the others I have."

"Listen, Stuart, the way the press are hopping up and down like a bunch of excited school children at the fair with this werewolf thing, they'll print whatever anyone takes into them. And when it all blows over, as the big fake it is, they'll point the blame for the public's hysteria on the smallest person they can find. The money-grabbing photographers! They'll blame you for adjusting the images to mislead people so you can make a few extra bucks."

Stuart stood up, and picked his folder up and saw himself out. Once he'd left, Dave picked up the phone. "Boss. I think we may have a problem."

"Keep an eye on him, Agent, and squash his photos."

Dave frowned at the thought of getting heavy on a kid. "Okay." He went and looked out of the window, spotting Stuart walking through the park. To anyone else, it would've just looked like a large green expanse, and if they really strained they might have seen the people as ants going about their daily business, but Dave could make out the squirrel's climbing the trees.

He set off in pursuit of his 'new to be' friend.

Chapter 30

"**I**'ll see you Monday, about midday,"

"Yes, sir. Enjoy your golf," Luke Spangler Jr said, as his dad left the office.

Luke Spangler Snr was the CEO of a large insurance/pensions firm in New York, having moved to Manhattan twenty-five years ago. They'd started trading in life and property insurance, but five years later added pensions to their portfolio and never looked back. With a vast turnover yielding a profit every year in the hundreds of millions, they were a very influential family in New York, then, with the tragic killing of the Williams' father and son, their business had exploded into the billions.

As Luke Snr jumped into the back of his limousine, which was waiting to take him to the airport, he shouted through to his driver, "You remembered to pick up my golf clubs from the hall, Kevin?"

"Yes, Mr Spangler," the chauffeur replied.

The car pulled away from the kerb, a moment later a black security van pulled away from the opposite side of the street.

As the limousine headed out towards JFK, Kevin was getting restless in the front. One of his passengers called through on the car phone, "Everything okay up there, Kevin? It feels a bit bumpy today."

"Yes, sir. I'll slow down. Sorry, sir."

"Don't slow down, we don't want to miss the take-off slot," the Spangler's bodyguard said.

As they left the island and headed towards the airport they stopped en route to pick up Luke Jr's children. They were going to be dropped off in Florida and spend the week in Disneyland.

With the children's mother's waving them off, the van that was following tailed the limo again.

They were a few kilometres from the airport when Kevin saw the van behind flash him three times, signalling for him to pull over.

"What's happening, Kevin," Luke Snr asked.

"I think we got a flat, sir. I'll just check the tyres."

As Kevin got out, the back doors on the limo were pulled open and a badge was shoved through the door.

"FBI," the voice shouted. "Please exit the vehicle."

Luke Snr's bodyguard relaxed and looked at his boss, "I'll go first, sir."

When they were both out, the man with the badge lifted his handgun and placed it against the bodyguard's head. The bodyguard reacted instantly, pushing the handgun out of the way. Swinging again, he planted the palm of his hand, in an upward motion, just below the man's nose. The man was unconscious before he hit the ground. Another man fired twice, killing the bodyguard and Luke Snr, instantly.

The kids, two girls, aged eight and nine, and a boy, aged eleven, started screaming as they were pulled out of the car. They were gagged, hooded and had their hands tied behind their backs and thrown into the back of a van.

"Where's my money?" Kevin demanded. He was shot in the leg, gagged, hooded and thrown in the back with the kids.

The men retrieved their buddy, who was still unconscious, and the van sped away.

One of the men rang a number. "We've got them."

"Any problems?" the voice said.

"Nothing we couldn't handle!"

When the van rolled into an old factory unit, a man sitting up in one of the old offices dialled the Spangler building.

Ten minutes later, the FBI were parking to the rear of the Spangler building. They were shown through to the service elevator and whisked through to the conference room on the ninetieth floor.

As they sat down, the phone rang, the room went quiet as an agent nodded at Luke Jr to answer it.

"Hello," he said, shakily.

"We told you not to inform the police. Now one of the hostages will die."

"No, please, not the children!" Luke Jr pleaded. As he spoke there was a shot, followed by terrified screaming. "What have you done?" he shouted down the phone.

"This time it was the chauffeur, next time it'll be one of the girls!" the man hung up.

Luke Jr slumped down in his chair and put his head in his hands. Suddenly the room started getting busy, and half of the agents left.

"We've got their position." Was all Luke Jr heard, as he was ushered out.

As they hustled down a service corridor at the rear of the building, the man in charge said, "There's a SWAT team on their way now. They'll be there in thirty minutes."

"Where?" Luke Jr asked.

"Brooklyn."

****

The SWAT team surrounded the building and waited for the word to go in. The commander spoke to Dave's boss on the phone and nodded. He turned to the radio operator and gave the word, "Go!"

They entered the building, silently making their way around the empty rooms. All the commander kept hearing was, "Clear. Clear."

Six minutes later, he got confirmation the place was empty.

"Yep. There's no sign of anyone. Orders?" the commander asked.

Just then, one of his men said, "Found a note."

"Hold one," he said as he waited for the Notre to arrive.

The commander relayed the message to Dave's boss.

'Now that's twice you've tried to catch us, so now the boy dies!'

"Shit! Clear up and stand down." Dave's boss ordered. As he said this, a scream came over the radio before it went dead.

The building exploded! The command truck rolled onto its side, killing a reporter who'd tried getting an early story.

"What the hell was that?" Dave's boss asked. No reply came back, so he asked again.

"The building just exploded!" the commander shouted through the crackle of the radio. "Get the fire and rescue trucks here!"

Dave's boss looked at Luke Jr, deciding not to tell him. "False alarm. They must have been tipped off again. You have a problem on the inside!" He turned to one of his men, "Get me, Agent Phillips."

Chapter 31

Across the other side of the park, Stuart had seen a couple of guys staring at a woman and pointing at a wooded area. Something in his head said this doesn't look right. He followed them, ready to catch it all on film.

Dave watched as Stuart hid behind a tree, watching the three guys walking along the path near the lake. He hung back to see how Stuart would deal with, what Dave could make out, was going to be an attempted mugging. He stood about a hundred metres behind Stuart but had no trouble seeing what he was doing. He went and sat on a bench and smiled at the young sleuth.

Dave watched as the young lady entered a sheltered part of the park, then watched as the two men started to jog up to her. He could hear the electronic clicking of Stuart's camera as he shot the scene. Dave got up and made his way over to the trees hiding the three people. He could see Stuart watching. Dave walked up to the two men as one of them held the woman in a neck hold as he kept watch. She looked petrified as the other one went through her bag.

"Go away, man!" the one watching, threatened.

The other man looked up and froze as Dave moved forward and grabbed his mate by the mouth and pulled him to one side, dumping him on the ground. The woman was about to scream when Dave put his finger to his mouth, "shush."

Dave glanced around, Stuart had moved into the tree area and was looking at him. The woman grabbed her bag and ran off. The two men regained their composure and approached Dave, pushing him in the chest and cursing.

"Motherfucker! Now you're going to regret getting in the way."

Dave put his hands up and pleaded for them to leave him alone, but they stepped in and started beating him.

Stuart looked on, willing Dave to change as he shakily held his camera ready. The two men finished off by kicking Dave down to the ground, then stepping on him. Dave whimpered and lay still. The two men went through his pockets and ran off.

Stuart watched, stunned. Dave groaned, struggling to stand. His face was bleeding and cut, he looked up, straight at Stuart and then fell down again.

The young photographer ran up to him and tried to help, but Dave shook him off. He staggered up, pulled a cloth out of his pocket and covered his face, then made his way out of the park, Stuart in tow.

As Dave approached the FBI building, Stuart stood back and watched him enter. Dave went in and sat down on one of the chairs in the lobby, his head in his hands, slouched over the side of the chair. Within moments he was surrounded by work colleagues all wanting to help him. They escorted him over to the lift and up to his office.

Stuart went through the pictures on his camera and frowned, turned and left.

In the lift, one of the agents said, "Doors closed, Dave."

Dave stood up and brushed himself off, collected his weapon and wallet from one of the five agents with him. "Do you think he went for it?" Dave asked.

"He looked pretty pissed off if that helps!" one of them said, working his jaw with his hand

"Are you okay, Mark?" Dave asked. "Sorry if I got a bit rough!"

"I'm okay. I was more worried about you changing."

As Dave walked up to his office, Brodie, his new secretary, handed him a message, she then put the handbag she was holding back in the lost property box.

"You alright?" he asked.

"Yes, thank you."

Dave looked at the message, turned, and went straight out to meet with his boss.

Chapter 32

"**W**hat's up, boss?" Dave asked, looking at the man with him.

"This is Luke Spangler Jr."

Dave shook hands. Something inside him growled.

"This morning his three children and their chauffeur were kidnapped on the way to JFK. Luke Spangler Snr and his bodyguard were shot dead. The chauffeur has now also been killed."

"Any leads?" Dave asked, looking at Luke.

"We've chased the phone call and have an address, but there's a problem. Someone's working on the inside of the Spangler building and tipping them off about our moves, so this is yours."

Dave nodded and went back over to Luke. He looked at him and sniffed, turned, nodded at his boss and left to speak with the commander of the SWAT team. Once he had the address, he set off to find Stuart.

"Grant, meet me at the Bronx Zoo."

"Where?" Grant gasped. "You ain't thinking of going in the wolf enclosure are you?"

"The Bronx Zoo," Dave repeated. "I'll see you there in an hour. Don't forget your camera."

As Dave sat outside the zoo, waiting for Grant to show, he sat thinking about the odour he'd picked up on Luke Jr. He couldn't place the smell, which bugged him! He thought about all the places he'd been and had come up with a blank.

Grant arrived and jumped into Dave's car. Dave looked at him, "What took you so long?"

"I went and had a chat with a few friends who've taken over the subway job old Don used to do. What's so important? Do the Penguins need a passport photo?" Grant joked.

Dave breathed in deeply, making Grant back up against the door. "Are you alright, Dave?"

"There's that smell again," Dave frowned.

Grant lifted his arm and sniffed himself.

"Take a few pictures of the wolves and get them printed off. I'll see you back at your place later."

"Have they got any wolves in there?"

"It's a zoo, isn't it? If not, a wild dog or something that looks close to a wolf."

"I could've got them off the internet," Grant huffed. "I could've been having a lazy afternoon by the pool with Max."

"I need a few photos with some buildings in the background. Try and get some that show they were taken in New York, okay?"

Grant shrugged, "Okay, but why can't you do it?"

"There's a certain young photographer who's following me. The last thing I want is for him to take a photo of me standing next to the wolf enclosure."

As Grant climbed out, Dave could hear the electronic shutter popping on Stuart's camera. He counted twelve shots.

He started the car and drove up to Stuart. "Jump in. I'll drive you home."

Chapter 33

Later that night, as Grant was printing off the pictures he'd taken, Dave huffed.

"What's wrong?" Max asked.

Dave looked at her and thought, Why not. "Max, have you ever found something but can't place where you'd seen it or smelt it?"

Max thought for a moment. "Yes," she said, staring at him.

Dave waited for a follow-up but she just sat there looking at him.

"Okay. How'd you go about finding out where it came from?"

"I don't usually let it phase me. I just tell myself I'll remember what it was when I do something."

Dave looked at Max for a moment, this time she picked up on the thought line.

"For example," she said. "If I'm struggling to remember something, like a name, I'll just tell myself, 'when I get home and put the key in the door I'll remember it'."

Dave looked at her for a moment and thought, I'll give it a go later, nothing to lose. "Thanks, Max."

Grant walked in with the pictures and handed them over. "They're not bad, even if I say so myself," Grant smiled.

Dave looked at them, going through until he found the one he wanted. "Perfect. Thanks, Grant."

"You're welcome."

"Can you send me the file with these in?" Dave handed him his email address at work.

"Sure. I'll send it over tomorrow."

As Dave drove down the drive, he stopped at the end and thought about what Max had said about the smell he couldn't place. I'm going to the diner tomorrow, it'll come to me then. He smiled and drove off.

The next morning at work, Dave spent an hour altering the pictures. Once he was happy he pinged them through to his boss.

His boss smiled and pinged a message back.

'Okay. Get me this Stuart guy and let's squash this now.'

Stuart was at his parent's house, having spent the night after a family get together, something he hadn't done since before meeting, Carrie. He was brushing his teeth when his phone buzzed, sending a crazy frog shrill through the house. His mum came in and muted it. "Please change that ring tone, it's driving your father insane!"

He nodded and smiled, breathing in the sweet scent of the pancakes and maple syrup breezing in with her. "Sure, mum." He picked the phone up and looked at the screen.

'I have some pictures you'd be interested in. Call.' He looked for a few seconds and wondered... "Pictures?"

"Hello."

"Stuart. It's Agent Phillips."

Stuart straightened up when he heard Dave's voice. "Yes?"

"I'd like you to come to my office. Let's say in, twenty minutes!"

"But I'm not dressed yet."

"Good, I'll see you then." Dave paused for a moment, "And bring your camera."

In the cab, Stuart started running through his head everything he'd done over the last few days, the police station, the park, the zoo. He couldn't think of anything where he might have stepped out of line.

Walking through the main entrance to the FBI building, the assistant at the welcome desk called him over and issued him with an ID badge, a set of instructions, and pointed him over to the lift.

When the doors opened, Stuart was ushered through to Dave's office. As Stuart entered, the door was closed. He turned and looked at it, he could see the silhouette of the man that had escorted him through the floor to ceiling blind covering it.

"Good morning, Stuart," Dave's boss grunted.

Stuart jumped as he turned and looked at the two men, Dave and his boss, standing in front of Dave's desk.

"I understand you've been following one of my agents, taking pictures, and now claiming he's a," Dave's boss chuckled and shook his head before he said the last part, "werewolf!"

Stuart looked at the two men and then noticed the three men standing in the corner by the coffee machine. He swallowed hard and nodded, unable to speak as his mouth had suddenly dried up. His hands began to sweat and he started feeling hot.

Dave sensed his discomfort, "Would you like something to drink, Stuart?"

"Water, please," he squeaked.

As Dave fetched him a glass, his boss asked Stuart to sit down.

"I have a couple of photos that might interest you," Dave's boss said, as Dave placed a glass of ice and a glass of water down in front of him.

Stuart took a mouthful of water and looked at the images on the table. He was putting his glass down when he realised what he was viewing. His hand stopped, holding the glass just above the table as he focussed on a picture of a wolf, and anther picture of Dave morphing into the Wolf.

He put the glass down and picked the photos up, moving his view from one to the other in quick succession. He stuttered,

"You knew? I was right." He looked up at Dave and saw him smirking.

"We faked these with a common web tool you can download. They've gone out on YouTube and Facebook. No one will believe you," Dave's boss said.

"Now, can we have your camera, please?" Dave asked

"No!"

"Are you sure?"

"Yes!"

"Okay. You're free to go," Dave's boss said. "Oh, and Stuart."

Stuart looked up, expecting him to say something along the lines of, 'don't let me see you again', or, 'next time we'll arrest you,' but all that was said was.

"Thank you for coming over and visiting us today. We always welcome the public who like to come and say, 'hi'."

Dave stood at his office window and watched as Stuart walked off across to the park. Stuart stopped and looked up at the building and then turned, disappearing into the shade of one of the tall horse chestnut trees, which grow in abundance.

"Do you think he bought it," Dave asked, "the mugging and the pictures?"

"Follow him for a few days," his boss said, whilst pouring himself a coffee. "See what he does. But I think we're safe."

Chapter 34

"**L**unch," **Dave thought,** as his stomach rumbled. Walking out of the building, he turned left and headed for the diner. As he walked along, he glanced over at the trees in the park.

Breathing in the heavy scent, from the sap and the pollen, he thought about Linda and the others out in the hills near the ranch. "I'll pop out there tomorrow," he thought. "Surprise them."

A couple of dogs came close to him, then cowered away, their tails between their legs as they hid behind their owners. Dave smiled to try and put them at ease.

As he walked in through the open door of the diner the smell of fresh bagels and ground coffee bombarded his senses. His mouth started watering before he'd even walked across the threshold.

"Hi, handsome," Iris greeted him.

Dave smiled and pointed at his usual chair. "Hi, Iris."

Once he'd ordered, he sat watching the people going about their business on the street. Scurrying around like ants. The only difference between what he was watching and the ants, is ants talk to each other!

As he sat drinking his coffee, a smell hit the back of his nose, which made him sit up. Coffee and money mixed. He looked around the diner at the people coming and going and zeroed in on a young man buying a large bag of cakes and four cups of coffee. A picture of the tunnel where he'd found all the crates with Jasmin came to him. Dave realised he knew the face, the man who stole his wallet.

The man's manners were non-existent as he demanded certain cakes from the display under the counter. Iris totally blanked his attitude and served him quickly, moving on to the next customer.

"That's the smell!" he thought. He left twenty bucks on the table, the meal only coming to twelve, got up and followed him out. He watched, frustrated as the man got into a car and drove off. He looked at the midday traffic and set off after him.

As he jogged along, about a hundred metres behind, he watched as it turned, he worked out he could take a short cut. Turning down a back alley he built his speed up. Dave felt the wind brushing his face as he jumped the bins and rubbish piles blocking his way. Bounding up to the first level fire escapes and jumping back down with ease. He thought of the guys back at the ranch running through the trees and smiled as he leapt through his own concrete jungle.

When he got to the far end, he stopped and watched as the car crawled past in the lunchtime traffic. Two in the front, one in the back, he thought, as he got his phone out.

"Boss."

"Yes, Dave?"

"I've got a lead on the Spangler case. I'll let you know where I am when I get there."

"Okay. I'll have the SWAT team on standby."

Chapter 35

Dave jogged along, avoiding people as he tailed the car. He hadn't even broken into a sweat but was looking forward to moving into less populated streets where he could stretch out again.

The car headed south, towards the Manhattan Bridge, but carried on and turned up onto the Brooklyn Bridge. Dave smiled as he approached. I've wanted to do this for ages, he thought.

He jumped up onto the overhead crossbeams and ran along, above the cars, loving the feel of the sea air as it blew his hair back. He kept as tight into the shadows as he could, but every now and then he'd see someone look up at him and stare, nearly rear-ending the car in front as their mouths dropped open or they mouthed some curse at him.

Because of the traffic on the bridge he'd reached the other side before the car. He stood next to a lamppost and watched as it drove by. The occupants paying him no attention as he chewed on a hotdog.

Dave followed the car towards the Red Hook district where he watched them make a turn into an old industrial area down by the docks.

The area was being renovated into prime real-estate property, with a marina, bars and shopping complex.

The car skirted a few derelict buildings, pulling up outside an old sewing machine factory. Dave moved forward, over to a fire escape ladder on the building next to the one they had pulled up to.

As he climbed the ladder, he heard a shutter open, the car revved a little and the shutter came down.

Moving up onto the roof, he skirted around the edge of the flimsy, rotting roof until he could see the door the car had used.

The gap between the two roofs was about five metres, "Easily jumpable," he thought, but the roof of the other building looked old. He scanned the area where he stood and spotted a wooden beam lying near a skylight.

Picking his way across the roof, testing each footfall, Dave went over to pick it up. Just as he got to it his legs disappeared from under him, he found himself hanging from a roof panel, twenty metres above the concrete floor. He watched as the rotten roof that had supported him, settled down on the floor below, dust billowing up around him and out through the hole.

As he hung there, he could hear the whole building creaking. As he looked up at his handhold, the roof appeared to be rippling.

Dave swung himself up and stood perfectly balanced on a length of timber. He looked at the building opposite as the walls around him started to collapse. The noise rising into a deafening collage of small explosions as glass broke, timbers snapped and brick walls all fell in on each other. He leapt towards the wall, landing and then springing over the gap in one bound. Landing on the wall of the adjacent building as the factory he was on continued to collapse in a heap of rubble, the dust and debris climbing up into the clear Brooklyn skyline. The smells wafting high into the sky, drifting over him, making him wince.

As he crouched, waiting for the dust to settle, he heard a door open below him.

"Shit, man!" the voice shouted. "The building next door just collapsed."

Dave recognised the voice as the guy in the diner. The door slammed shut, and he heard a commotion coming from below him. He zeroed in his hearing and listened as they discussed moving somewhere safer.

"What about the three kids?" one of them asked.

"We'll find somewhere else to take them first, then we'll come back for them."

"But what if the building collapses before we get back?"

"Then we'll move on and get some more kids."

"Get the kit together, we'll move out in thirty minutes. Jeff, make sure the kids can't get out."

Dave counted the different voices, five of them. He got his mobile out.

"Yes, Dave?"

"Down on the old docks in the Red Hook district. There are five of them and they're talking about the kids. One of them has just gone to check on them."

There was a silence for a few moments. "SWAT can't get over there for at least forty-five minutes. We can get there in twenty. We'll come up the water route, meet you down on the quay."

"Okay. They're moving out in thirty minutes," Dave added.

Chapter 36

Dave worked his way around the parapet surrounding the roof, staying as close to the edge as he could, he didn't want to bring this building down... He got over to the quayside and waited for the police launch to show. Fifteen minutes later, he spotted the white bow wave from a small craft coming towards his position. He counted seven bodies on board.

Two water officers, four of the agents who knew about him, and his boss.

As they got closer, they killed the flashing light and drifted up to the quayside. Dave climbed down and briefed them.

The four agents took up their positions around the building, covering the exits. The two water officers manned the dinghy and waited for the SWAT team.

When they were in position, Dave's boss got a click on the radio from each one of them. He returned two clicks and tried the door. To his surprise, and Dave's, it opened.

Dave entered first and moved to one side, his boss going to the other, closing the door quietly behind them. His boss wrinkled up his nose at the smell, blinking a few times as it hung heavy in the air. Dave just frowned as they worked their way over to a stack of packing pallets.

Dave's radio clicked quietly. He looked at his boss, who nodded at a pile of boxes a few metres away. The two of them listened for a moment, and then made their way around the stack, over to where they could see the car and two people talking. Just as they got closer, one of the other agents stumbled, knocking over a broom. The two men drew their weapons, and fired at him, bringing him down. The other three agents engaged. A shot hit one of them in the shoulder. As he fell, the other two dived for cover, working their way round to Dave and their boss.

Dave's boss quickly let off a shot, hitting one of them in the chest, killing him instantly. In the same instant, Dave lifted his gun and fired at the other one, watching as the guy's head exploded in a crimson and grey cloud.

They carefully crept forwards, at a crouch, to recover their wounded colleague. When they reached him, Dave knelt down and felt for a pulse, he looked at his boss and shook his head.

"Shit!" his boss cursed. He looked over at the one who'd been hit in the shoulder and nodded at the door, the agent looked around and made his way out.

As the four of them watched for any movement from the mezzanine floor above, a shot splintered off the box next to Dave, sending them all dropping to their knees, scrambling for cover.

Dave thought for a moment, then said, "Boss!"

"Yes?"

"Don't shoot me, okay?"

Dave's boss turned and looked at him and then at the others, they all shrugged.

"I'm in complete control on this one, it is not like the last time, okay?"

"Now is not the time for riddles, Agent," his boss grumbled.

"Just don't shoot me. You're all perfectly safe."

When he said, 'perfectly safe' his boss and the other agents looked at him and backed off a fraction, already scared about what might happen.

Dave undressed and folded his clothes, placing them on the floor in a neat pile. He took a deep breath, "Remember, you're all safe!"

As Dave knelt, a shot rang out and a bullet planted itself into the wall behind them, instinctively one of the agents went to grab Dave, thinking he'd been hit, but immediately recoiled. Nearly falling out from behind the shelter, he muffled a shriek with his hands.

Dave lay on the floor. He twisted, bones protruded out of his body and then folded back in on themselves, the open wounds healing instantly. His skin turned to fur and his face caved in and then extended. This all took less than five seconds. When he'd finished he stood between his boss and the agent and growled, low and long. The noise filling his teammate's heads, echoing through their chests as they tried to steady their breathing.

The wolf looked at each of them in turn and trotted off towards the shooters. The agents looked at each other, Dave's boss shuddering at what he'd just witnessed.

As the factory fell quiet, the agent's heard a growl and then a shot being fired. They all looked at one another, then behind themselves, their eyes wide with a mixture of fear and awe, reflexively huddling closer together as the two men above, screamed.

They watched as the wolf trotted back to where they were standing, blood dripping from its snout! It rolled over and transformed back into Dave.

As he stood, one of the agents said, "Dave, your blee...."

Dave looked down as the wound closed and healed.

"Shit!" the agent finished.

He got dressed, "Clear, boss, but there's one man missing."

His boss's mouth opened and closed a few times before he managed to squeak, "Good work, Dave."

Dave led them over to a room he'd passed when he attacked the two men. "In here," he pointed. "I heard some whimpering, it sounded like the kids."

Dave's boss signalled for one of the agents to get the door open.

Inside, they found the three children who'd been kidnapped and the missing man. He held a gun to the youngest girl's head. Over in the corner, a man lay down on his side, not moving.

Dave, his boss and the two agents fanned out across the room, all keeping the man in their sights.

"Let the kids go!" Dave's boss demanded.

The man was clearly nervous. Dave could feel his fear and sense his panic. He recognised him as the one who'd been in the coffee shop earlier. "Did you enjoy your coffee?" The man looked at him, confused.

"Iris makes the best coffee and cakes in Manhattan," Dave said, trying to calm him down. "Why don't you put the gun down and let the kids go?"

The man edged over to one of the windows and took a quick glance out. Below him was an open garbage skip, half full of paper.

"Back off!" he shouted, "or I'll kill the girl!"

"Okay, okay. Stay calm," Dave said, gesturing with his hands. "We'll back off." Dave looked at his boss, "Stalemate."

His boss looked at the other two agents and nodded at them to leave. They slowly edged their way over to the door. As they reached it there was a shout from outside the window, the man looked down without thinking. Dave saw his chance and leapt forward, morphing in mid-air. The man saw something move and lifted his handgun, firing two shots whilst moving off to the side, pushing the girl forward. The wolf's flight took it past the man and over the girl. She froze as the wolf tried to twist to alter its direction. Fearful, the man turned and fired two more shots, hitting the wolf squarely in its flank. The adrenaline pumping through the wounded creature blanked out the pain. The wolf turned as soon as its paws struck the ground, springing forward and leaping towards the man. This time it found its mark and clamped its huge jaws around the man's throat. It bit down and ripped the man's head away from his shoulders in one fluid movement.

The children screamed and ran for the door, straight into the arms of the two agents. They swiftly moved them away, covering their eyes to shield them from the carnage behind them, and waited for their boss.

The wolf circled the body twice and then stopped, it lifted its huge head and howled. Cursing, his boss covered his ears and stepped back towards the door.

The wolf morphed, and Dave staggered to the wall, naked and exhausted. His boss shouted for the agents to leave the children outside the room and help him with Dave. They ran in, their weapons raised, ready to fire, then stopped in their tracks, as they looked at Dave. He was holding his sides together, to stop his insides falling out! As they watched, Dave's boss was removing his jacket and trying to get him to lay down.

Dave pushed him away, "Don't touch me! Stay away from the blood!"

His boss flinched and looked down, his shoes were in a puddle of it. "Shit!" he cursed, as he jumped back and forced them off with his feet.

They all watched in silence as Dave's side healed and the blood dried away. Dave walked forward and held his hand out, his boss handed him the jacket and just stood, staring.

Outside, the SWAT team had turned up and were taking the kids to safety. They were dirty, scared, and hungry. They'd been beaten, and the boy's arm hung at a jaunty angle, clearly broken.

The man lying down in the corner was the chauffeur. He was covered in a black swarm of flies. Maggots were falling off his body, feasting on the rotten flesh. He'd been left where they'd shot him, obviously in front of the children.

One of the agents came back into the room, he was as white as a sheet and looked as if he'd been sick.

"Are you okay, Agent?" his boss asked, looking at him.

He looked over at Dave, his eyes wide with horror. He stuttered, "The other two are dead, sir."

Dave's boss had figured that one out already. "Go and get some air. Guide the rescue truck over and get them to send a chopper as well." As the agent turned to go, his boss followed up with, "I want this area sealed off."

"Yes, sir. Also, the SWAT team found a reporter taking pictures on the roof opposite."

Dave turned, and said, "That'll be Stuart."

"The reporter who had the pictures of you?" Dave's boss gasped.

"Yes, sir. I recognised the voice when he shouted. He's probably got a camera full of me morphing."

"Take him to my office, Agent Johnson. I'll sort this out once and for all." Dave's boss growled.

The agent nodded, looked at Dave again and left.

Dave went over and checked the pockets on the man he'd attacked. "My badge," he said, holding it up to his boss.

Chapter 37

When the children were safely in the ambulance, and the bloody remains of the two men had been shovelled up and bagged, Dave's boss turned to him, "Dave. We need to talk. My office, seven pm."

Dave nodded and looked over at the other agent who was staring at him. "What about Agent Johnson?"

"He'll be there as well, and so will my boss."

Dave nodded, then said, "I'm going home to have a shower."

****

When Dave walked up to his apartment, his senses came alive. He was dog tired, but the wolf inside him stayed alert twenty-four-seven. Standing a little way down the corridor, he breathed in deeply, picking up a scent he recognised. Dave smiled and walked in, and was straight away jumped on by Linda and Janet. Clayton and Frances were sat in the corner.

"Guys," Dave smiled.

"Thought we'd come and see how the city slicker's doing," Clayton said. "Especially after what Linda told us about the eclipse."

"How are you, Dave?" Frances asked, concerned.

"Good. Just very tired. But suddenly very awake now you guys are here," Dave beamed, hugging them both.

Linda made drinks for everyone, whilst Dave went to his bedroom and got changed.

Sitting around and talking, Dave replayed the events from the other day when the eclipse caught them out. "We'd forgotten all about it, we killed six agents," he paused and looked at Linda, then dropping his head, "one of them was, Grace."

"The mess around the office was intense," Linda added.

"The reason we're here, Dave, is to come and meet your boss. We've decided to come clean!" Clayton said.

"You'll have every freak in the city gunning for you. We won't make it out of the city alive!" Dave said.

"This either ends today, or we start a new chapter," Clayton said, patting Frances on the leg.

"I've got to go back in and see my boss later, at seven, his boss is going to be there. Why not come in and talk to them first, see where they want to take it?"

Clayton looked at Frances and shrugged.

"Sounds good," Frances said.

"There's something else I need to tell you guys. I scratched someone who was trying to blackmail me. My boss knows as he watched the aftermath of it all. She only half-changed, and when she did, she went crazy. She ate her own foot before she died."

"Ate her own foot!" Clayton gasped.

Frances covered her mouth in shock. "Where is she now?"

"They, the FBI, took her to a secure bunker just outside JFK. They're autopsying her now."

"We need to find out why that happened," Clayton added.

At six-fifty pm, Dave and the others walked up to his work building, Clayton deciding Dave should go and speak with his boss first.

Outside his office, Dave knocked. As he did, he was greeted by four Special Forces personnel, they stood either side of him, weapons drawn.

"Erm! Good evening?" Dave stuttered. As he turned around and looked at them, he noticed four little red dots centred on his chest. When he looked up, he spotted the gunmen they belonged to, stationed around the far walls of the open-planned office.

"Come in, Agent. Have a seat," his boss called.

The four men followed him and took up positions around him. Dave looked at them, and grimaced, "This isn't necessary, sir. You're all perfectly safe."

His boss looked at him and then at his boss. "Sir, this is Agent Dave Phillips."

"How's Linda, Dave?"

"She's fine, sir. Thank you."

The head of the FBI stood up and walked over, holding his hand out. Dave stood, and the four Special Forces personnel moved closer as he took his hand and shook it.

"Well done, young man, well done."

"Thank you, sir," Dave said, somewhat confused.

"Now tell me all about this... power of yours!"

"Before I do, I need to tell you something." Dave looked at his boss, "Sorry for not informing you first, sir, but it's just come up."

Dave's boss looked at him and then offered him coffee. "What is it, Dave?" he asked.

"Linda's downstairs, and so are a few more of my friends."

When he said, 'And so are a few more of my friends' his boss looked nervous. "What do these 'friends' want?" he asked. "Is there going to be any trouble?"

"No, sir."

"Should I leave?" the head of the FBI said.

"No, sir. We're here to meet you and speak to you about a proposition. Just one thing though," Dave said, looking at the soldiers around him. "These guys are really unnecessary."

"Well they're staying, Dave," his boss butted in. "Where are these friends of yours."

Chapter 38

Ten minutes later, Dave, Clayton, Frances, Janet and Linda were standing in front of his boss and the head of the FBI. Just for good measure, two of the snipers joined them. All the soldiers had their weapons trained on the team.

"Good to see you again, Linda," The head of the FBI said.

Linda stepped over to him and gave him a hug, "Good to see you too, James. How's Debra?"

"She's fine. Speaks about you." He turned to the others and greeted them.

Clayton stepped forward and offered his hand, "Good to meet you, sir."

James hesitated, but then reached out and shook Clayton's hand. "Good evening. I understand you have a proposition for me?"

"Yes, sir," Clayton said. "But we have to ensure one thing first," he said, looking around at the weapons zeroed in on him.

"Okay. What?" James asked.

"That no one shoots us!"

Dave's boss and James both looked at them.

Dave's boss said, "Is this going to be the same as in the warehouse?"

"Yes," Dave said.

"Oh!"

James looked at Dave and gestured for them to sit down. "Okay, Dave. Let's have it."

Dave stood and turned to the agent and the soldiers, and asked them to stay perfectly calm, "Don't react to anything. Everyone in this room and the two soldiers outside are perfectly safe. This will only take two minutes."

Outside, the two soldiers heard, "Oh my God!" They looked at each other, and then back at the door, their fingers covering their triggers.

Inside, James and Dave's boss, the agent and the soldiers stood, their mouths open, eyes bulging and all totally frozen to the spot.

Once everyone was dressed again, Dave motioned for the gang to sit. "We'll give them a couple of minutes," he said, smiling. Inside, Dave felt as if a big burden had been lifted off his shoulders, but something right at the back of his brain told him it was just the beginning. He looked at his boss, who then looked at his boss. They both waited for him to react.

"Erm...well...Okay!" is all he said. He looked at the soldiers who were just staring at Dave and the others. The soldiers then looked at their boss and, as one, lifted their weapons up and put the team back in their sites.

"We need to know what happened to the woman who died, you took her to a bunker for an autopsy," Clayton said.

James gave Dave's boss an inquisitive look, "Well?"

Dave's boss wrote an address down, and handed it to Dave, saying they should meet him there in forty-five minutes.

As Dave and the others were leaving, walking through the open-plan office towards the lift, one of the Special Forces men called Janet back.

"Ma'am," he said.

Janet looked at him and smiled, "Yes?"

The others had stopped and were now watching the two of them.

The soldier fidgeted as he stood in front of her, "Would you like to go for a coffee?" he asked.

"After what you've just witnessed?" Janet said.

The soldier smiled, "Can I pick you up later when we've finished here?"

She nodded and held her hand out for some reason, to shake his. He looked down at it and then shook it.

"Date!" Janet said.

The soldier stood up straight and saluted her and the others. He turned and gave the thumbs-up to his mates, who smiled.

Janet walked over to the lift, bouncing slightly from what just happened. The others just stared at her and then back at the soldier.

Chapter 39

On the outskirts of JFK, Dave and Clayton stood at the front of Clayton's F150 Velociraptor.

"Nice truck," Dave said, admiringly.

"Thanks. We needed something to carry the groceries!"

As they stood chatting about the tyres and its pulling power, the beams from a Jeep bathed them in light as it rolled up. There were three soldiers on board, two of them getting out.

One of them came forward and opened the gate. "Agent Phillips?" he asked.

"That's me," Dave indicated. "Hi, guys."

The soldier pointed his flashlight at Dave. "We need to check your vehicle, sir."

"Feel free," Clayton said. He tapped on the bonnet and the women got out.

The soldier glanced inside and then asked for the bonnet to be lifted. He looked around the engine compartment before nodding at Clayton. "Thank you. Follow me, please."

They were escorted over to a hangar door. As they approached, the doors opened, exposing a brightly lit space about the size of a tennis court. As they parked up the doors closed, they were then taken through to a room off to the side. When they were all in, including the three soldiers who'd escorted them, the door closed automatically and the whole room started to drop slowly.

"Wow! It's all very transformers, isn't it?" Janet said, smiling.

The lift had taken them down to an underground complex. The whole area turned out to be a maze of rooms, some conference, others sleeping, eating, a gym, and others clinical.

Dave's boss and James met them and escorted them through to see the autopsy.

"It's not a pretty sight," Dave's boss turned and warned them.

"We're werewolves!" is all Dave said.

He looked at him, and shrugged, "Of course."

As the door opened and they entered the room, the smell of embalming fluid filled their heads. The room was clinically white, with a row of windows at a height for people to watch what was happening on the table in the centre. A collection of cameras and lights hung from the ceiling above it.

On the table, was what looked like a huge skin-coloured tablecloth, with a turkey carcass sitting in the middle. As they got closer it turned out to be Lynn's body. All that was left was the rib cage, the skull and the internal organs.

"Where's the rest of it?" Clayton asked, looking closely.

"That's it. There is no more," Dave's boss said.

Just then, the door opened and the lead pathologist joined them at the table. "Good afternoon," he said, studying them. "I'm Professor Graham."

Clayton turned and shook his hand. "Where's the rest of the body, Professor?"

"That's all that was in the box. We were hoping you could possibly tell us what may have happened," he said, staring at Clayton's face.

Clayton looked at Frances and then the others, he shrugged and raised his eyebrows. "Any thoughts?"

The others just carried on looking at the body, shaking their heads.

The group were shown through to a large conference room. The walls were covered in SMART boards and computer screens, with a huge central projector stationed in the centre of the ceiling.

Dave, Clayton and the others were sat around a large table. Dave's boss and James were sat opposite.

"Okay," James started. "How's this going to work?" he looked at Dave as he asked.

"You now know about us, so let's work together," Dave answered.

"You mean like some superhero team of Avengers?" James scoffed.

"No! I don't mean like some bunch of superheroes. We're not here to save the world and rid it of all evil. We're here to show you we're not a danger to anyone. We simply want to be left alone."

"So why did you reveal yourselves to us? We wouldn't have known any different if you hadn't come forward," Dave's boss said.

Clayton broke the silence in the room. "We're willing to help, but not to become depended on. Just to help out as and when you really need us. But we need something back in return."

James looked at him for a moment. "What do you want?"

"We need you to help us make our shelter impregnable, so no one can get in, and we can't get out," he said. "We'll also need somewhere here to change if we can't get back."

The two bosses looked at each other and smiled.

"Deal," James said.

Chapter 40

Dave pulled his boss to one side as they were leaving the complex. "I know who organised the kidnapping."

"I'm listening."

"Luke Spangler Jr."

Dave's boss looked at him, "So one of the richest men in Manhattan, hell, New York, organised the kidnap of his own children and the shooting of his father. Are you crazy?"

"I picked up on a scent on one of the men at the warehouse. I was trying to work out where I'd smelt it whilst I was following them. It wasn't until they moved the car inside the building that it came to me."

"Still listening," Dave's boss said, walking back into the shadows.

"The shutter going up reminded me of the underground garage at the Spangler building. When Linda and I came back the other day, we passed their building. I spotted Luke Jr talking with some men by the entrance to the car park. He was leaning on the wall near to the mechanism for the shutters, with one of the men from the warehouse. And when I met him in his building, the scent was on his hands."

"Okay. But we're going to need more on him than a smell. Find a way," his boss smiled.

"What happened with Stuart?"

"He's been told, in no uncertain terms, he's to keep a lid on what he saw. He's signed the Defence Secrets Act. And it's been explained to him, if he breaks it, he'll not see the light of day again."

****

The next morning, after Clayton and the others had left to go back home, Dave booted up his iPad and accessed his files on Luke Spangler Jr.

As he left the building, Stuart was waiting.

"Morning, Dave."

Dave looked at him and frowned. "If you want a scoop, then follow me," he said, suddenly realising he could help out.

They got in a cab. "The Spangler building, please," Dave said.

Walking in through the lobby, Dave showed his badge to the receptionist and asked to speak with Luke Jr, expecting to be told he wasn't there.

She ushered him over to the lift, giving him a pass for the conference room. "Mr Spangler will be with you shortly," the receptionist said, smiling at Dave.

Figures, Dave thought. "Thank you."

She looked at Stuart and was about to ask who he was, when Dave said, "He's with me," as the doors closed.

As the lift doors opened, Stuart gasped, "This lobby is bigger than my whole house!" He stepped out onto the deep pile carpet and breathed in the scent of expensive leather coming off the sofas lined along the wall. The hall was bright and exuded a feeling of wealth and power. Paintings of the Spangler men adorned one wall, with ornate ornaments standing on occasional tables placed neatly between the sofas opposite.

"Follow me," Dave ordered.

As Stuart followed him through a set of large, dark oak doors he marvelled at the plain office furniture in a neat semi circle in the middle of the space. He spotted an iconic print on the far wall, stopping to look at it, he gasped as he realised it was the original painting.

Dave sat over by the window and looked down at the people walking along the road, ninety floors below. He could just about read the headline on one of the trashy rags on the newsstand.

'Lock Up Your Daughters! Randy Wolf On The Rampage!!' He shook his head and smiled.

Stuart came and sat with him, "Seen anything interesting?"

"What! From up here?"

Stuart frowned and turned back, marvelling at the room he was sat in.

They waited no more than a minute before Luke Spangler Jr entered. He came over and shook Dave's hand and looked at Stuart. "Press?" he asked.

"Freelance," Stuart said.

"Wait outside, please."

Stuart looked at Dave and sighed as Dave nodded.

"How can I help you, Mr Philips?"

"Not. Have you found my father's killer?" Dave said, watching for a reaction.

"I've been led to understand you have two people in custody, Mr Philips. The children are safe and being cared for at home. But, have you found my father's killer yet?"

"Yes!" Dave announced. He watched as Luke Spangler Jr recoiled slightly from the news. It was very slight, but what gave it away was the increased heartbeat and the sudden onset of an enormous amount of sweating.

"Yes?" Luke replied. "What do you mean, yes?"

"I've found out who killed your father!"

Luke stood and listened as Dave explained.

"You wanted to be the top dog. But because of all the money, and the good living the old man, your father, Luke Spangler Snr was enjoying, he started to improve with age instead of, well, dying! After you arranged to have the Williams' taken care of, you took over their business interests and assumed your father would retire and leave you in charge. Now I have someone downstairs who's willing to testify you and your late father were locked in a bitter power struggle for control of this business, but he was a far better businessman than you could ever hope to be. So you arranged a little trip for him to go and play some top-class golf with a few top professionals on the Augusta course for the week. And for your children to go to Disneyland whilst he was there." Dave stopped and looked at his face. He could see the elevated blood pressure levels running through the veins in his forehead. "Got you," he thought. Dave focussed on the recording machine in his pocket, the sound of the mechanism working calmed him as he waited for Luke Jr to pop. He could also see Stuart's hand pushed through the opening of the door, a microphone pointing directly at them.

Luke pulled a handgun from his jacket pocket and pointed it at Dave, "Shame no one will be around to hear that, Agent Phillips." He tensed his arm and started to put pressure on the trigger but turned his head slightly when he heard the door squeak as Stuart moved to get a picture.

It was all Dave needed. He reacted. Before Luke Jr knew what had happened, Dave had sprung forward and moved the weapon away and twisted him around, holding him in a neck lock.

Stuart had switched the camera to video mode and recorded everything Dave did and said. Dave knew he could count on Stuart's reporter nose, and read Luke Spangler Jr his rights, word for word from the card he took out of his pocket.

****

Down at Precinct Thirteen, Dave finished writing up his report on the arrest of Luke Spangler Jr and handed it over to the station officer. He posed briefly for the lone pressman to take his photo and then went and got a coffee.

****

"Well done, Dave," his boss said. "The pictures look good as well. It seems as if you've done Stuart a favour. I hear he's now being head-hunted by The New York Times!"

"If he sticks around and doesn't try and mess up, he'll get some good pictures in the future as well."

"The late Mr Williams' chauffeur has been released and is now back with his family. Luke Spangler has confessed to setting him up."

"He got a deal. Didn't he?" Dave said, looking at his boss.

"He's a very powerful man, but he won't last long. He's made quite a few enemies over the course of the last few days, and now they know what's happened he won't be around New York anymore. Mr Williams' widow has promised to make sure the chauffeur and his family will be looked after."

"What about the children?"

"They're now back with their family, and their mother has filed for divorce, she'll get it. Now, I'll see you tomorrow and we'll go over these plans Clayton left for the secure building. Nine am, Dave."

"Yes, boss."

Chapter 41

Later that evening.

Dave opened the door to the diner. Iris was sat in a chair watching Sky News. "Evening, Iris."

She smiled, as he walked up to the counter. "Evening, handsome. Out late tonight?"

"Couldn't sleep. Busy?" he said, looking around at the two other customers in the corner. He nodded over at them.

"What can I get you, Dave?"

"Strong coffee, please." He watched as she went back into the kitchen to grab some fresh beans for the machine. He waited for the door to close and got up and left. On the counter, where he was sat was a ten dollar bill wrapped around a note.

When Iris returned, she looked around, the couple in the corner nodded at the door. She picked up the money and opened the note. Read it, and put it in her pocket. She turned to put the bag of beans down and stopped in her tracks. She reread the note. A tear appeared in her eye as she took the message in. Politely asking the two customers to leave, not taking any money from them, she locked the shop up and went around the back of the café, to her car.

As the note had described, there on the front seat, hidden in the dark, was a black briefcase. Iris opened her door, her hands physically shaking. She climbed in and sat behind the wheel. Looking up and down the alleyway, to make sure she hadn't been followed, she locked the doors, something she'd done ever since being attacked twenty years earlier. She leant over and popped the two latches on the case.

She gingerly lifted the lid a few inches, looked at the twenty dollar bills and closed it again. Looking up and down the alley once more, she lifted the lid up all the way. Placed in a row were ten bundles of notes. Lifting one up, she flicked the edge, fanning her face, and placed it back down. She smiled and started her car.

Dave stood back in the shadows and watched her drive away. "Have fun, Iris," he said to himself. He turned and looked at the back door to the diner, and thought, "It'll never be the same."

Read on for a sneak preview of the next book,

3. Red Dawn.

Part of the **MW** series.

Chapter 1

With his heart beating hard, the adrenaline pumping through his veins, Dave stared at what was unfolding in front of him. His body twitched, wanting to join the action just a few metres from where he crouched. The field was alive with testosterone, he could smell the excitement all around, and he could taste the fear as it flooded his senses.

   Calls bounced out across the arena as the away fans watched the possibility of going home under a cloud. He glanced up at the scoreboard, all tied with five seconds left on the clock. He watched as the referee bounced the ball towards the shooter, catching it, he smiled and winked at the opposition as they stood pulling faces. Dave felt the tension around him thicken as the shooter went still. He tensed as he watched him look up at the backboard. The shooter's face straightened as the concentration spread through his body, he focused on his goal, whispered to God, and bounced the ball once. His Achilles tendons released just enough energy to flex his ankles, lifting his body the few centimetres required to aid the path of the ball towards the hoop. The atmosphere stilled as every eye watched the ball, necks craned, as if they were aiding in its quest to find its sanctuary.

"Sounds like another victory," Bill smiled, as he stopped and listened to the roar rising from the Knicks stadium. "Get the spare bottles up from the cellar," he said, looking at his one member of staff, "tonight's gonna get busy!"

Another long night, Jane frowned. And I betcha a buck he tries to wriggle out of the extra pay! "Get it yourself. I quit!" she cursed, as she threw her towel down and headed out the door.

"Looks like you're gonna be busy tonight!" his only customer smirked, lifting his glass for a refill.

"See you at six," Bill called, as the door slammed. He sighed as he poured another tumbler of bourbon, this time leaving the bottle on the counter.

Jane huffed, looking up and down the street, smiling briefly as the noise coming from the stadium rose again. Probably doing a lap of honour, she mused. She never really enjoyed the crowds that went with sports, although she excelled in a crowded bar, flirting with the customers, getting the big tips. At college, she was a loner, an ugly duckling who didn't come into her prime until a year after leaving. Being overweight, she would disappear into her studies, not that it did her any good. She flunked all her exams after a couple of the "popular girls" took it upon themselves to befriend her then dump her the day before the first test. She left California the next year to find her fortune in the Big Apple, but like a lot of people, she crashed out on the job front. After sleeping rough for eight nights, and sinking to eating out of the dumpsters behind a couple of the fast food restaurants, she ended up working in Lou's bar. That was three years ago, she now had a little place down in Brooklyn, it wasn't big, but she called it home.

The heat was rising in the city, and the breeze moving in off the Hudson had all but stopped. Jane had instantly broken out in a sweat when she left the air-conditioned bar. Removing her shirt, she tied it around her waist leaving just a flimsy, dark slip covering her tanned body, showing off her curves perfectly. She checked her reflection in the bar window and smiled at her latest addition. She'd had a tattoo of a dolphin added down her left side, its snout starting just below her left clavicle, its body curving around the swell of her breast and back over her flat tummy, its flukes dropping either side of her navel. When she worked late at the bar all she wore was a sports bra and spandex leggings. With her long, blonde hair tied back in a ponytail, her new body art was a much talked about subject with the regulars.

Making her way home, she glanced in the window of the hotel a few buildings down. She waved at the bellhop, Aaron, giving him a friendly smile. He was thirty, ten years older than her, but Jane liked that. He'd come in the bar on Friday evenings and say, "Just shaking off the rich shit!"

She'd spent a few happy nights with him in his apartment, nothing serious, just sex, she mused, but he had a great body and made her laugh. She didn't drive, so she either walked or got the bus. As she'd forgotten to pick up her wages when she walked out of the bar, today was a walk day.

As she made her way along the street, getting farther away from the stadium and the noise, she dreamed of the trip she had planned. Saving for the last three years, she planned and emailed old friends who'd moved away. Her dream was to travel through Europe, spending time in each place she came to. If it worked, she'd stay a little longer, and if it really worked, she'd settle down. First, she had another twenty thousand dollars to save, taking her entire savings pot up to twenty-five thousand. But she really loved body art!

The roar from the home fans was deafening as the ball cleanly found the hoop and dropped through the net. The score went up one point, to fifty-six - fifty-five, as the claxon sounded a fraction before the final whistle. The floor vibrated as excited people stampeded down to the sideline, and spilled over onto the court. Dave jumped up from his seat and joined the celebrations sounding throughout the arena. He was being hugged by a fan who'd made her way down, pushed by the wave of people who wanted to touch their heroes. She was jumping up and down, screaming.

"Erm! Hi," Dave said, raising his voice to be heard over the noise.

"Hi!" she squealed. "Don't you just love this game?"

He nodded and smiled, giving up on talking. She looked at him, and mouthed, "Do you want to go for a drink?"

He shook his head and went to squeeze past her. She dropped her arms, wrapping them around his waist, and ran her hands up and down his back, squeezing his butt slightly, "Are you sure?" she mouthed, the tip of her tongue brushing her top lip.

Dave pointed at his ring finger and smiled. She shrugged, returned a disappointed smile, and disappeared into the sea of fans. He shook his head and made his way over to the exit. As he left with the throng of spectators heading home, or wherever they were making their way to celebrate, he removed the gold band he'd started wearing to fend off overbearing women. Not that he minded, but sometimes he thought, you just need some alone time.

As he made his way through the gridiron layout of streets that make up New York, he smiled at the simplicity. Why all cities couldn't be laid out like this amazed him. "If it could work for the Babylonian Empire and New York, then it could work for everyone," he'd say at parties. The worst experience he'd ever had was in London. He'd gone on a lad's weekend with a few colleagues when they'd all finished university, spending four days in London instead of three after getting hopelessly lost.

As he rounded the corner towards a little Italian restaurant he'd started frequenting with Linda, he focused on a young woman looking in the window. He noticed that, apart from the blonde hair, her build was much the same as Linda's. He smiled as he thought about being with her again in a few days. As he got closer, he could see she was reading an advert for a job vacancy. He admired the tattoo running down her side, and nearly commented on it, but noticed Max and Grant waving - he was meeting with them to discuss their wedding plans.

As Dave opened the door, he glanced at the young woman. Catching her looking at him, she blushed. He smiled, she returned the compliment, brushing her hair out of her eyes with her index finger.

"Hi, Dave," Grant said, standing up and shaking his hand.

"Hi, Dave," Max greeted, blowing him a kiss.

"Hi, guys. Been here long?"

"Long enough to order a bottle of house." Drink, Grant gestured with his hand.

"No. Thank you." Dave looked up, and a waitress came over. "Water, and an OJ, please."

"Yes, sir," she said, looking at him for a fraction longer than she wanted.

"So, best man. Got a speech ready yet?"

Dave nodded and tapped his pocket to show that it was written and awaiting its day. "How are you, Max?" he asked. "Not bored with the old man yet then?" he chuckled.

"He's my hero," she said, ruffling his hair. This time it was Grant's turn to blush.

The door chimed again, a few people, including Dave, looked up to see who'd walked in. The young woman went over to the bar and pointed towards the advert. Dave heard her asking about the position. She was taken through to the back. Ten minutes later, she re-emerged, smiling. Dave spotted her coming out, raised his glass, and mouthed, "Congratulations." She smiled and left. A few moments later, one of the waitresses removed the poster. Dave smiled to himself, and thought, this could get interesting.

Dave eventually left and headed home, jumped straight in the shower, changed, then left and headed for the woods.

If you'd like to know the history of Manhattan Wolf, read the **Scalpturio series**.

You can do this at:

barrybuckinghambooks.com

Sign up for my newsletter to receive updates on new releases.

About the author:

Now being three quarters of my way through my third twelve year career, first one serving in the Royal Air Force, then running my own business as a driving instructor, and now working for Vivacity driving the mobile library, I decided it was time for me to put pen to paper and get the book out of me that, apparently, everyone has in them. I write in the military thriller genre, releasing my first book, Scavenger Hunt, back in 2012, as well as the supernatural genre. Since then I have had two more children that keep me very busy and fit.

Have a look at my web site: barrybuckinghambooks.com for the other books I have written.

If you've enjoyed my work, please leave a review on the site that you purchased it from. All independent authors look forward to hearing about their books, the good ones and the bad!

Here's to my next.

18705406R00078

Printed in Poland
by Amazon Fulfillment
Poland Sp. z o.o., Wrocław